WHERE CHRYSANTHEMUMS BLED

AISHNEE SINGH

Copyright © Aishnee Singh
All Rights Reserved.

This book has been self-published with all reasonable efforts taken to make the material error-free by the author. No part of this book shall be used, reproduced in any manner whatsoever without written permission from the author, except in the case of brief quotations embodied in critical articles and reviews.

The Author of this book is solely responsible and liable for its content including but not limited to the views, representations, descriptions, statements, information, opinions and references ["Content"]. The Content of this book shall not constitute or be construed or deemed to reflect the opinion or expression of the Publisher or Editor. Neither the Publisher nor Editor endorse or approve the Content of this book or guarantee the reliability, accuracy or completeness of the Content published herein and do not make any representations or warranties of any kind, express or implied, including but not limited to the implied warranties of merchantability, fitness for a particular purpose. The Publisher and Editor shall not be liable whatsoever for any errors, omissions, whether such errors or omissions result from negligence, accident, or any other cause or claims for loss or damages of any kind, including without limitation, indirect or consequential loss or damage arising out of use, inability to use, or about the reliability, accuracy or sufficiency of the information contained in this book.

Made with ♥ on the Notion Press Platform
www.notionpress.com

For the ones still standing—
The ones who kept going when they failed,
when truth fractured,
and when silence screamed louder than anything else.

This is for you.
For surviving.
For Being—
and never letting the world go.

—With all my pages,

Aishnee Singh.

Contents

Preface

It began with a tattoo I couldn't forget—
The Serpent and the Dagger.
I didn't know what it meant at first (and maybe, neither should you).
One coil. One blade.
One truth that twists. One end that cuts.
That image sparked a world—
Where truth slithers, lies cover.
Where a girl doesn't just survive the myth—
She becomes it.
That's how "Where Chrysanthemums Bled" was born.
From a symbol.
And from Lilith Kaelyn Aurelious—
the dagger she never saw coming.

Acknowledgements

To my parents—
Mrs. Geetika Singh & Mr. Raj Bir Singh—
for your endless love and belief in me.

To my aunts and family—
Ms. Sangeeta Gupta, Ms. Aneeta Gupta, Ms. Neelima Gupta, Mrs. Monika Gupta, Mrs. Pushpa Singh, and Mr. Sanjay Bharti, Mr. Avinash Gupta & Mrs. Madhuri Gupta—
for your constant support and care.

To my dearest friends and loved ones—
Sarthak Bhaiya, Advik, Jivitesh Bhaiya, Bunny, Aradhya, Jhanvi, and Namrata—
thank you for the laughter, encouragement, and late-night conversations that kept me grounded.

To my Dadi and Nani—
for your quiet strength and blessings that follow me in every step.

To my respected teachers-
Mrs. Huma Akhtar and Mrs. Deepika Shukla.

And my heartfelt gratitude to—
Canva, Google Documents and Notion Press and every tool that helped bring this story to life.

For your unwavering support and extended assistance—this book carries a part of all of you.

With love,
Aishnee Singh

Trigger Warning (tw)

Where Chrysanthemums Bled

xi

This book contains themes and content that may be distressing or triggering to some readers, including:

- Violence & Murder
- Blood & Gore
- Trauma & PTSD
- Death & Grief
- Psychological Manipulation
- Betrayal & Deception
- Suicide & Self-Destruction
- Torture

Reader discretion is advised. If you are sensitive to any of these topics, please proceed with caution.

Prologue

I held white chrysanthemums that were stained by my blood drenched hands. I opened my eyes as the beam of sun rays fell on me.

Getting up with a jolt, I turned toward the large mirror by the side, my gaze locking onto one entity—staring deep into her black irises. The one who stood behind those weary eyes. The one buried beneath the weight of unspoken words and unfinished thoughts. I searched for something—recognition, understanding, a glimmer of the person I used to be before the weight of the past settled on my shoulders.

I was beyond miserable or sad. I couldn't even put it into words. Tears? No, no tears fell. Why? Because I felt trapped within them.I knew I lost something but the dimwit I was looking at was oblivious as to why to cry. As though every emotion, every unspoken scream, had congealed into something thick and suffocating, weighing me down. The tears weren't absent because I was strong—they were absent because I had exhausted even the ability to cry.

I lifted my hand, pressing my fingers lightly against the cold surface of the hospital mirror, tracing the outline of a face I barely recognized. Was this truly me? Or was I merely the remnants of a person who once felt, once lived? My breath fogged up the glass, a fleeting mark of my existence, disappearing before I could hold onto it.

Outside, the wind roared, rattling the window panes. The world moved on, indifferent to the battles waging in my head, the voices muffled deep in it. I closed my eyes for a moment, steadying myself. The weight of every yesterday before this, threatened to crush me. And yet, I stood.

Even if I didn't know who I was anymore.Even if the reflection before me was just a stranger.

I stood with the innumerable questions my chest tightened and eyes blurry before I felt hitting to the floor surrendering to my weak knees

CHAPTER ONE

Echoes Of The Forgotten

"On the bright morning of the 20th this month the Chrysanthemum building from the celeste group of companies was inaugurated, in the presence of Ms. Lilith Kaelyn Aurelious -"The news continued. "Shut it", I snapped at Aaron. He handed me my Einspaner before he left the room, allowing the corporates to come in.

"Are all the representatives present here Mr. Mariano", I questioned the man across the table who was roughly the same age as Eve.

"Yes, my subordinate, he's missing",he continued "...-not that he's significant, afterall I am here for the signings how can anyone outshine me Ms. Kaelyn"

"Archaic," I muttered with a smirk, that remained hidden by the paper I had in my hand.

"Huh?"

"The idea of this report's Archaic... does not fit our standard,"I continued "....-consider redrafting," getting up from the chair.

"But how? On such a short note",he continued.

"This paper doesn't meet the standards my company upholds ," I reverted.

"But we worked hard on this ," he said almost with a hint of confidence.

I smirked, tapping the report. "Oh, you worked hard? Cute. Too bad we reward results, not attempts. Try again."

"But-"

"Leave, we reward competence not complacency Xavier," I intervened.

"How can you address your ally's representative that way?" he reprimanded.

"You lost that title the moment you dismissed your subordinates' authority."

"Now leave before I make you regret this... Xavier," I said

"Schedule a meeting with the others that were shortlisted "

A meeting was convened four days later. We were about to sign the closing deal with a company when a man entered and sat opposite to me. He exuded a powerful aura

When suddenly my breath hitched ,my head felt dizzy and I felt a wave of memories hit me when my gaze fixed on a man, who looked inexplicably similar to 'him'. I don't understand why, but my body reacts before my mind does—my hands shake,breath shortened, and for a second, I feel the sting of a bullet *again*. I snapped out of all thoughts when a hand tapped my shoulder, I turned to see Eve with her brows raised.

I sat at the conference table and my gaze drifted towards that man a few times while my fingers fidgeted with documents on the table. I felt uneasy with him in the same room, a strange air lingered.

My PA, Aaron Rudwick—better known as Aaron—caught my averted gaze. Knowing my workaholic nature, he immediately asked whether something had caught my attention or if I had spotted a flaw in the report.

I had joined this company two years ago on the recommendation of my previous employer and was appointed CEO despite having no prior experience. At the time, my life was unraveling, and I couldn't afford to let this opportunity slip away. I suffered from memory loss because I was shot by my previous company's rivals.

The day went by as anticipated.

I reached my mansion and threw my coat and shoes as I crept to the couch.

"Remember me, even though I have to go, Remember me", a man sang in a deep voice, the song from Coco.

I got up with a jolt, it had to be him, was this my previous company's rival?

As the sun took over the darkness my head, still hurting from the effects of insomnia, spun in a million directions. I sat on my office chair, "Aaron, get white chrysanthemums for me," I ordered as he left after nodding. "It's interesting, isn't it? When you realize how selfish you are to judge the course and mood of the elements surrounding you by the number of tears shed the previous day, how we see the world through the lens of our emotions. The same wind that brushed past me yesterday feels as if it is slamming the windows now, laughing in mockery," I thought to myself with a smirk just when Aaron stepped back in the cabinet saying, "Saw that dream again, didn't you." Gently placing the Chrysanthemums in the flower vase.

I nodded. Aaron was not only my PA but also my best friends' elder brother, they too were by themselves and we three resonated like a small family in the world of our own. The first time I saw him, he appeared unassuming—almost forgettable. He wore thin, rectangular spectacles, their frame a muted silver that caught the light just enough to make his sharp eyes glint with something unreadable. His dark hair, though slightly tousled, was neatly parted, giving him an air of meticulous precision. He appeared to be a serious individual which he was, but was softer to his family and I often confided my worries in him and Eve or Evelyn Rudwick, my best friend. She too worked here – as the Manager of the marketing team.

Aaron alone understands why I always order chrysanthemums, those are the only fragile threads connecting me to my past. He then told me with a smile, "Whenever I go there, the florist asks if I'm attending a funeral."It has always been about death—my existence, my name, my belongings, and the only past self I can recall. I merely nodded, forcing a hollow smile. He was trying to lift my spirits, but some things are too heavy to be carried away by words.

"Aaron, what's the name of the man who signed the closing deal yesterday?" , I asked with a curious concern.

"I'll look into it," he replied, assuring me.

I was never told the minute details of how I lost my memories, because I was the only one who knew me before that and the company I worked with closed after the mass killings at their North building and I trusted them but my dreams didn't show me the setup of an office.

I am sane but I have injured myself brutally sometimes when I get these psychotic episodes.

About ten days ago.

I woke up and something in me was already broken.

I don't remember walking to the mirror, but I do remember what I saw in it—

Not me.

Her.

The other version. The one with blood on her hands and no apology in her eyes.

I laughed.

It echoed through the walls like a warning. Like I'd already done something I hadn't yet.

I went straight to the drawer.

The knife I kept in the false bottom wasn't there.

Because I'd already taken it out last night.

Because part of me knew this was coming.

I walked to the tub.

Turned on the water.

Didn't wait for it to even fill.

I let the hot water fall from my head to the bathtub's floor.

I needed the burn.

I dragged the blade across the edge of the porcelain—not my skin, not yet—just the tub. Just to hear the sound. That scream of metal against something pretending to be pure.

Then the sink.

Then the wall.

I painted with it. Not red yet. Just scratches. Just rage.

And then I saw her—me—*again.* In the window now. Smiling like she knew how this ended. Like she was daring me to catch up to the monster I already was.

So I did.

I slashed the wallpaper.

I tore open the closet.

I smashed the only picture frame of mine and me until my fingers bled.

I wanted to rip the past out of the walls.

I wanted to bury the future before it betrayed me.

The next thing I remember is sitting on the floor.

Breathing heavy.

Hands shaking.

Blood—mine—maybe.

Laughter still in my throat.

Tears nowhere to be found.

And the knife?

Still warm in my grip.

Because when the dream ends, I begin.

And Lilith Kaelyn Aurelious doesn't wake up quietly anymore.

Aaron was the first to witness this scene I created and thus, Eve and Aaron have booked with a psychiatrist this Saturday and have forced me to visit it.

Saturday arrived with the wink of an eye.

I arrived at the tall, grey, and seemingly lifeless building well before my appointment. The structure loomed against the overcast sky, its glass windows reflecting nothing but the emptiness above. A place like this wasn't meant to comfort. It was meant to analyze, to dissect, to fix what was broken—as if minds were machines that could simply be rewired.

Eve accompanied me, her presence steady yet distant. I could feel her watching me, though she said nothing. Maybe she thought this was the right thing to do. Maybe she was right. Maybe she just wanted me to stop waking up in the middle of the night, gasping for breath as if my own past was trying to strangle me.

The receptionist barely glanced up before waving me toward a door at the end of the corridor. No waiting. No distractions. Straight to the point.

I hesitated at the threshold, gripping the handle. The cold metal sent a small shiver up my spine. My stomach twisted, but I forced my face into something impassive, something that wouldn't give away how much I hated being here.

"You good?" Eve asked quietly.

I nodded once. A lie so effortless, I almost believed it myself.

The psychiatrist's office was suffocatingly neat. Muted beige walls, wooden shelves filled with meticulously arranged books, and a desk too clean to belong to someone who spent their days digging through people's fractured minds.

Dr. Everett sat across from me, an older man with sharp eyes behind thin-framed glasses. The kind of person who could strip your past down with a single glance, peeling away the layers you desperately wanted to keep hidden.

"Lilith Kaelyn Aurelious." He said my name like it was a puzzle piece he was trying to fit into an unfinished picture.

I sank into the chair, crossing my arms. "I assume you've read the file."

He gave a slow nod. "I prefer to hear things directly. Files don't tell me how you feel."

I smirked, but there was no humor in it while my brows frowned. "Feelings are overrated."

A flicker of something crossed his face—interest, amusement, maybe even challenge—but he remained unreadable. He was already dissecting me, and I hadn't even said a word that mattered yet.

He glanced at the notes in front of him. "Eve mentioned you've been experiencing recurring nightmares."

I shot Eve a look. She didn't flinch.

"Not just nightmares," I muttered, gaze dropping to my hands. They were more than that. "It's like... pieces of something I can't reach. A past I should remember, but don't. And when I wake up, I feel like I've lost something. *Again*."

His pen scratched against paper. "Describe them."

I hesitated. Not because I couldn't, but because I didn't want to.

"...It's never the same scene, but the feeling is," I finally admitted. "There's always blood. Always a coldness in my bones. Sometimes I'm running, sometimes I'm falling. And sometimes..." My fingers curled into my palms. "There's someone singing, but I never see their face."

Eve shifted slightly beside me.

"Do you recognize the voice?" he asked.

I shook my head. "No. But I think—" I exhaled sharply. "I think they want me dead or that they died."

A long silence.

Another note scribbled.

"Do you believe your nightmares are memories, Lilith?"

I met his gaze. The question was too direct. Too pointed.

I forced a slow breath. "I don't know."

But I did.

He tapped his pen against the paper. "What do you feel when you wake up?"

I swallowed. "Exhausted, Weary,Dread."

"Dread of what?"

"Not knowing." My voice was quieter than I intended. "Not knowing if it was real."

He leaned forward slightly. "Lilith, your mind is trying to tell you something. Recurring nightmares—especially trauma-induced ones—are often the subconscious's way of resurfacing buried truths."

I didn't respond. My fingers dug into my sleeves. I know my PTSD, I want medicines not a therapist.

"If these are memories," he continued, "then it's possible something—or someone—is keeping you from remembering."

My breath hitched. The room felt smaller, tighter.

"Do you think you're ready to find out what's hidden in your dreams?" he asked.

Yes.

"But our brain tends to forget the past we don't remember, it's better if they stopped-" he continued

"I am quite busy actually, I'll send my Assistant to fetch the medicine, you can hand me the prescription," I said getting up from the chair that trapped me through this entire time and walked out the door frame and then out the building, without glancing.

"What was that? " Eve asked.

"I was protecting myself"

"How?", she continued.

I paused then looked at her... confused.

"These dreams keep me alive, Evelyn," I retorted.

"You know who you are. What you were. You know how to exist. I hate it.

I hate my life. These dreams. The people I don't remember, the places that feel familiar but remain just out of reach. I detest it all."

"-But you know what's worse?"

"-I can't end it."

"-And do you know why?"

My voice wavered, but not from weakness. From anger—the kind that boiled beneath my skin, clawing at my ribs, demanding to be let out. My breaths came uneven, shaking with something between fury and despair.

"Hope." The word was bitter in my mouth. A cruel joke.

"Every time I get these stupid dreams... I wish—" My voice cracked. "Oh, how I wish I could see the lifeless body I feel beneath my hands. The bullet that rips through my life, my dreams, myself. And the man—" I squeezed my eyes shut as the image flickered in the darkness behind my eyelids and my three fingers hit the temples of my head at the gun wound. A silhouette. A song. A feeling so familiar it made my stomach twist.

"The man who is so obsessed with that freaking song—"

I stopped. I couldn't breathe.

That's when I felt it.

A touch.

Not firm, not reassuring—just there. A loose embrace.

Evelyn's arms around me.

The sensation sent a shiver down my spine, not from comfort but from something I couldn't name. A weird feeling encapsulated me, curling around my ribs like smoke. This wasn't warm. This wasn't a relief.

Then—

A lump formed in my throat.

I didn't remember how to cry.

Yet, here I was—falling apart in my own way, in the arms of the one person I could trust.

And for some reason, that terrified me.

Then I said, "I don't I just don't want these dreams to be", my voice came back to its normal pitch.

"Evelyn, I want to know who I am, I really wish to, "I said with a genuine smile while Eve just remained silent. It was enough to indicate that she was dissatisfied but wanted to let me be.

Her silence infuriated me, I didn't hate her. I hated how I felt helpless, how I needed to be looked over, how I needed someone by my side. This feeling was not intended but embedded in me, I was detestably short tempered but not impulsive, maybe in the past but not now, and trust me even though I seem to have lost it, I don't regret anything after I've done it... isn't that not being impulsive? The only thing I liked about myself.

"I know you didn't know me before Eve," I said, widening her eyeor maybe I did, but not this version,"I know I didn't know any of you and–" I paused "It's not that I don't trust you, but Evelyn, I know better than anyone that I didn't, ever work at a company-"

I continued and just as I could let out the next word, I looked at her eyes. They were the manifestation of the inner emotions, she looked... terrified.

I stopped and turned to my car, "Get in Evelyn, we'll talk later".

I reached home after dropping her off.

I had an unknown obsession with hot weather. Maybe one of the other threads connecting to my past, whenever I felt this overwhelmed, I submerged myself in water at lethally high temperatures, it didn't burn me, it calmed me, my burnt heart.

I laid on my bed facing the ceiling and woke up to the noise of a gunshot.

There was a man getting shot, I jumped to save him, he died in my arms *again* but it was different today, I saw him..

A square jawed man, long eyelashes, bruised face... he looked tall, above 6ft for sure.

"Non, pas toi... pas toi, Astrid." I screamed my hands dripping with sweat, I reached out to the glass "Ca c'était quoi," I mumbled in a language I could understand but not...

My eyes widened. I gripped at the glass by my side, it fell and shattered at once due to the sweat accumulated on my hands.

I got up and my feet fell on the shattered glass piercing through my heels but... the shock hit me so hard that it overshadowed it.

Getting hold of my keys and putting on my coat. I set off my hands often, losing grip of the steering wheel. My head felt the sting.

CHAPTER TWO

I AM LILITH?

"Why in the world do I know French..., Evelyn? Care to explain", I asked on call at 3AM pressing the accelerator of the Mercedes Benz S class with all the anger I held in, I knew it couldn't be that I loved Chrysanthemums out of nowhere, my obsession with hot water, working in a non existing company and now what... I knew how to speak French.

I typed in the password after driving all the way to her place like a maniac. She was sitting on the main hall's couch. "Why Eve?" I paused then with disappointing look, "I need to know, Eve"

Evelyn didn't look surprised to see me. The room was dark yet the lamp provided light enough to see her dainty figure. She was sitting on the couch, her fingers lazily drumming against the armrest, her expression eerily calm—too calm. As if she had been expecting me. As if she knew this moment would come.

Her gaze flickered to the clock on the wall before settling back on me. "Three in the morning, Lilith. You couldn't wait?"

I scoffed, slamming the door behind me. "You're joking, right?" My voice dripped with disbelief. "You knew this was coming. You knew I'd figure it out—bit by bit, piece by piece. And yet, you just sat there, waiting for me to lose my mind."

Evelyn exhaled slowly, sitting up straighter. "What do you want to know?"

I stepped forward, my breath still uneven from the drive. "Why do I know French, Evelyn? Why do I know things I shouldn't? Why does my life feel like some half-finished puzzle with missing pieces that everyone but me can see?"

She stared at me, and for the first time since I had known her, she hesitated. Just for a moment. It was brief, but I caught it.

I narrowed my eyes. "You knew."

Evelyn sighed, standing up. "Sit."

"No."

She shook her head, muttering something under her breath. "Fine," she said. "You want the truth, Lilith? You're not ready for it."

I laughed, but it was hollow. "Oh, that's rich. You think I'm not ready?" I stepped closer, lowering my voice. "Try me."

Evelyn took a slow sip, watching me over the rim of her glass. Then, finally, she spoke.

"You're asking the wrong question."

I frowned. "What?"

"You keep asking why you know French," she said, setting the glass down with a quiet clink. "Why don't you ask who taught you?"

My blood ran cold.

Something inside me twisted painfully, a memory—no, a whisper of a memory—surfacing like a ghost just beyond my reach. A voice. Soft yet firm. Instructing. Correcting. Teaching.

"Who..." My throat felt dry. "Who taught me?"

Evelyn tilted her head, watching me as if she were testing me, waiting to see if I could put the pieces together myself.

Then she simply said,

"Your brother."

Silence.

The world tilted, the floor beneath me no longer steady.

My brother.

The one I couldn't remember. The one who had been taken from me. The one whose absence had left a void so deep that I had spent every waking moment trying to fill it with something—anything.

I clenched my fists. My nails dug into my palms, but I welcomed the pain.

"You're lying," I whispered.

Evelyn shook her head, stepping closer. "I'm not."

I swallowed hard. My head was spinning.

"If my brother taught me," I said, my voice dangerously quiet, "then why don't I remember him?"

Evelyn hesitated again. A flicker of something—guilt, maybe—crossed her face before she masked it with indifference.

I stepped forward, my heartbeat thudding in my ears. "Eve." My voice trembled, rage barely contained. "Why don't I remember him?" with the utmost fury I felt in ages.

She exhaled through her nose. Then, she met my eyes.

"You know what to give me that phone number."

"Huh?" she said with a puzzled look tilting her head sideways.

"Oh, don't ," I said while moving my head side to side "I know you know someone from my past Eve, the..the..." I stuttered choosing my words carefully

"The one you always talk to away from me," she give me a puzzled look and I snapped

"Don't Eve... Astrid," I said a name that felt so known yet new, so close yet so far, so habitual, it... it was embedded in my memory.

I couldn't contain it, the rage, the fury. Looking at me like that, Eve took her phone out and moved her fingers over its surface then, looking up she gave me a stern look, just then my phone pinged, "Go look for the past you've forgotten Lilith," she let out a deep sigh, then continuing ",trust me there's no going back from it.No peace"

I sighed. As if I had been peaceful earlier. The man in my dreams was Astrid?

My breath uneven, my fingers withdrawing and reaching out to the blank screen of my phone, I slowly entered the password and opened Evelyn's 'View one time' message, a single number, I looked up.

"Call it," Evelyn said.

"And walk in another lie?" I said with a frustrated look on my face.

Eve was the only one who stood by me through my lowest. But it did not mean I could trust her blindly.

I stared at the phone screen, the message from an unknown number flashing coldly against the dark background. A single contact. A single name.

Vincent.

The name felt like a weight in my mind, unfamiliar yet somehow significant. Evelyn was watching me carefully, her fingers tightening around her glass, as if bracing for my reaction.

I looked up at her, my throat dry. "Who is Vincent?"

Evelyn exhaled, placing her drink down with deliberate care.

My pulse spiked at the name. Astrid. The man in my dreams—the one who felt so real yet so distant, like a ghost haunting the edges of my memory. But Evelyn said he was dead. So why did Vincent matter now? Wait, before why his right hand man, why couldn't she say PA or something.

"And why is he calling me?" I asked, my voice quieter now, laced with something I didn't want to acknowledge—dread.

Evelyn ran a hand through her hair, sighing deeply. "Because, Lilith..." She met my gaze, her expression unreadable. "He's been waiting for you."

A shiver ran down my spine.

The phone vibrated again in my grip, as if on cue. My fingers hovered over the screen before I finally took a breath and swiped to answer.

The voice on the other end was smooth, accented—French. Calm, yet laced with something sharper underneath.

I gripped the phone tighter. "Vincent?"

A low chuckle. "So, you do remember something."

My stomach twisted. "I don't know you."

"No," he agreed. "But you should."

I glanced at Evelyn, who was watching me with the same eerie calm, as if she already knew how this conversation would unfold.

I turned away. "Why are you calling me?"

Vincent hummed thoughtfully. "You're asking the wrong question."

I exhaled sharply, frustration bubbling. "Then what the hell should I be asking?"

A pause. Then, his voice lowered. "Calm respect me, I am your only family"

My breath caught. The room suddenly felt colder, my grip on the phone unsteady.

"Come to France, Lilith."

I swallowed hard. "And if I don't?"

Another pause. Then, quietly—almost gently, he said,

"Then you'll never know the truth."

The line went dead.

I pulled the phone away from my ear, staring at it like it might give me answers on its own. My heart pounded so loudly I could hear it in my ears.

France.

I looked at Evelyn. She didn't speak, didn't try to convince me. She didn't need to.

I already knew.

I was going.

"How's he my family, Eve?" I asked, squinting my eyes.

"He is the other brother"

"I have two brothers?"

Gosh, at first I thought my family didn't exist but what's this, this family tale sounds straight out of wattpad.

The very next moment, I knew.

"Book my tickets for France, Aaron," I said on call, gripping my phone a little too tightly.

"Huh? For when?" His voice was groggy, thick with sleep.

"For today."

A pause. Then a rustling sound, probably him sitting up in bed.

"What in the world, Lilith? Why are you telling me only now?" He sounded irritated, but I could also hear the concern laced in his words.

I exhaled sharply, rubbing my temples. "Because I just decided. I'll be there by five."

A beat of silence. Then, more rustling. "Five? Are you serious? Do you even have your passport ready? Your luggage? What about work—?"

"Aaron," I cut him off, my voice sharper than I intended. "Just book it."

He sighed, clearly trying to rein in his frustration. "Fine. Direct or with a stop?"

"Direct."

"First class or business?"

I rolled my eyes. "Does it matter?"

"To you? No. To me? Yes. Because if you're gonna call me at three in the morning to make last-minute international travel plans, I at least wanna know if you'll be sleeping in a reclining seat or suffering in the economy."

I pinched the bridge of my nose. "Business, then. Just get it done, Aaron."

There was a long sigh on the other end. "Got it. I'll send you the details soon. But Lilith—" he hesitated, "France? Why now?"

I hesitated too. Just for a second. "I have some business handlings, but book the flight under some other name and tell me that"

I lied with a straight face as always.

I deflected. "Just book the freaking ticket and also a hotel under not my name, Aaron."

I hung up before he could press further.

By the time I arrived at the airport, my mind was a tangled mess of thoughts I didn't have the patience to untangle. The cold air of the departure hall did nothing to calm the heat of anticipation—or was it dread?—settling deep in my chest.

I went through security on autopilot, barely registering the people around me, the murmurs of travelers, the distant beeps of scanning machines. My grip on my boarding pass was tight. Too tight.

Aaron's message flashed on my screen.

Flight confirmed. Paris. Terminal 3. Gate 14. Safe travels, Lilith. Don't do anything stupid.Theodore.Hotel lieu de confort

I almost laughed.

My flight was called, and before I could second-guess anything, I stepped forward.

Somewhere over the Atlantic.

I hadn't slept.

The hum of the aircraft was the only constant as I stared at the screen in front of me, the little plane icon inching closer to its destination. Paris.

I tapped my fingers against my armrest, Evelyn's words circling in my head. Go look for the past you've forgotten, Lilith. There's no peace in it.

It wasn't unfamiliar. It felt... buried. Tucked away.

I clenched my jaw, my reflection in the dark plane window staring back at me.

Vincent had called. He had answers.

I was going to get them.

No matter what it cost.

Paris,"Charles de Gaulle" Airport.

The moment I stepped off the plane, the scent of the city hit me—crisp, cold air laced with something I couldn't quite name. It was foreign yet familiar all at once.

My phone buzzed.

Vincent: Welcome home, Flower.

Home.

I wasn't sure if I wanted to laugh or run.

CHAPTER THREE

FLOWER.

On the phone-

Lilith- Why?

Vincent- I thought you liked it.

Lilith- Seriously? Flower.

Vincent- Chrysanthemums maybe.

The moment he texted that word something stung again. 'ils devraient atteindre leur place'(they should reach their place)

Why'd I want to say that of all things? It was perhaps motor memory.

I checked in and the first thing I did was submerge myself in hot water.

I heard someone curse.

Just then, something hit me—like a pang, sharp and sudden. My fingers twitched. My throat tightened. The sound rang in my ears, but it wasn't just from now. It was from before.

A voice. Rough. Angry.

I flinched. Why?

The scent of something bitter—alcohol? The sharp clatter of glass breaking. My breath came short, chest tightening.

"Useless"

Who said that?

The present blurred at the edges. A flicker of something too far to grasp. A shadow in my mind.

I hated cursing. I always had. But why?

Back at the hotel-

The weight of exhaustion pressed down on me. My body felt heavy, my mind hazy. I barely remembered making it to the bed before sleep dragged me under.

And then—

Pain.

Not mine. Not now. But then.

I was small. Fragile. My hands trembled as I gripped the edge of something—was it a table? A chair? The room felt too big, the shadows stretching long and unfamiliar.

A sharp sound cracked through the air. Skin against skin. A gasp. A choked sob.

"You think you are worthy of this meal"

Her voice.

A fist tightening around my arm, yanking me forward. The scent of perfume, too strong, masking something sour underneath.

"How many times do I have to tell you?"

Another blow. I recoiled, but there was nowhere to go. The walls blurred. My breath came in short, panicked bursts.

I wanted to scream.

I couldn't.

I woke up with a jolt. My chest heaved. The room was dark, but the past still clung to me—hot, suffocating. My hands shook as I curled my fingers into the sheets, grounding myself.

It was just a dream.

But it wasn't.

It was like the other dreams from my PTSD. It felt real and experienced and I woke up exhausted but this was the first time I saw something apart from 'Astrid'

I couldn't rest anymore. I just got up and stood. The air in the room felt heavy, pressing down on my lungs, thick with something unseen. I forced a breath in, then out. My fingers curled at my sides as I took a shaky step forward, as if testing whether I was still in control of my body, whether I was still here.

The silence was deafening. Even in the dark, the shadows seemed to shift, stretching toward me like whispers of a past I wanted to ignore. My mind felt raw, exposed. It wasn't just a nightmare. It was a memory crawling its way out of whatever locked place it had been buried in.

I reached for the lamp on the nightstand, but my hand hesitated above the switch. Did I really want to see? Did I really want to confront whatever was hiding in the dark corners of my mind?

Another breath. Then I turned it on.

The dim glow bathed the room in weak, golden light. The bed was a mess, the sheets tangled from my restless sleep. My pillow was damp—sweat, I hoped. I ran a hand over my face, fingers brushing against my temple, where a dull ache pulsed. The remnants of the dream refused to fade.

I saw it. Felt it.

The sound of something sharp cutting through the air.

The sting that followed.

A voice—a lady.

I winced as the fragments flickered through my mind, too scattered to grasp but strong enough to leave a lingering pain in my chest. She had been angry. I didn't know why. Maybe I had done something wrong, or maybe she just needed something—someone—to take it out on.

I had forgotten this, hadn't I? Or maybe I had just chosen to.

A sickening feeling settled in my stomach. What else was there? What else had I locked away?

I stumbled toward the dresser, reaching for the water bottle I had left there the night before. My hands trembled as I unscrewed the cap and took a sip, but it did nothing to soothe the dryness in my throat. I needed air.

I grabbed my phone, ignoring the time flashing on the screen. It didn't matter. I couldn't sleep now.

The apartment felt eerily empty as I stepped into the hallway. The floor was cold beneath my feet, grounding me in a way my own thoughts couldn't. My fingers found the light switch, and the overhead bulb buzzed to life, flooding the space with sterile brightness.

I exhaled.

I was here. Now. Not there. Not then.

Still, the echoes of my dream—of that memory—remained, lingering like a bruise beneath my skin. I pressed a hand to my forehead, shutting my eyes for a moment.

Then, my phone vibrated.

I jumped, the sudden sound slicing through the silence like a blade. My heart was still racing as I glanced at the screen.

Vincent.

The name sent a different kind of chill down my spine.

I hesitated before answering.

"Lilith," his voice was low, steady. "Come to-."

My grip on the phone tightened.

I didn't respond right away. I couldn't. I was still trying to pull myself out of one nightmare, and now I was walking into another.

Vincent sighed on the other end. "You know you have to."

I did.

Another memory—another truth—was waiting for me there.

And this time, there would be no turning back.

I didn't recognize the place.

Paris should have felt foreign, but it didn't. The streets, the scent of rain on cobblestone, the distant hum of a violin somewhere in the distance—it was familiar, yet distant, like a song I had once known but forgotten the lyrics to.

My head still throbbed from the dream. I had walked for nearly an hour, trying to shake off the lingering weight of it, but the unease clung to me. It wasn't just about my mother. It was about the realization that there was more—more I couldn't remember.

And now, there was him.

The café wasn't anything special. Dim lighting, wooden tables, the faint aroma of coffee mingling with cigarette smoke near the entrance. I scanned the room, then spotted him.

Vincent.

He sat near the window, fingers wrapped around a cup of espresso, his gaze fixed outside as if he were looking for something—or someone.

Me.

I took a breath, steadying myself before walking over. The chair scraped against the floor as I pulled it out, sitting across from him.

For a moment, neither of us spoke.

He finally turned his head, his eyes—sharp, assessing—meeting mine. The resemblance was subtle, but it was there. The same high cheekbones. The same shape of the jaw. But his expression held something I wasn't sure I had—a guarded coldness, a wariness that came from knowing too much.

"You look just like him," Vincent said finally, voice quiet but firm.

I stiffened. Him.

My brother.

The one I couldn't remember.

I swallowed, my mouth suddenly dry. "You knew him."

He nodded. "Better than you did."

A sharp pang hit my chest.

Vincent leaned back, studying me. "You really don't remember anything?"

I shook my head. "I didn't even know I had a brother until recently."

Something flickered in his expression, something unreadable. "Then why are you here?"

"'cause someone called me here?"

Vincent exhaled, setting his cup down. "And you think I have the answers?"

I tilted my head. "You do, don't you?"

A pause.

Then, he smirked—just slightly. "You're more like him than I thought."

I didn't know what that meant, but I wasn't sure I liked it.

"Tell me about him," I said, keeping my voice steady.

Vincent's smirk faded. He looked down at his cup, as if searching for something in the dark liquid.

Then, after what felt like an eternity, he said—

"He you, you know."

I gripped the edge of the table.

A memory stirred—just a whisper, just a flicker. A hand ruffling my hair. A voice, warm but distant. Laughter, muffled by time.

It was gone before I could hold onto it.

"I don't remember," I admitted.

Vincent looked at me then, something softer in his gaze.

"You will," he said. "And when you do—" He paused, voice dropping lower. "It will ruin you."

I didn't look away. "Then I guess I don't have a choice."

His lips pressed into a thin line. Then, finally, he nodded.

"Then let's start at the beginning."

Vincent exhaled slowly, setting his cup down with an almost deliberate grace. The ceramic clicked against the table, the sound far too sharp in the heavy silence. He didn't speak right away. Instead, he studied me—his gaze not unkind, but cautious, like a surgeon about to make the first incision.

I held my breath.

"You were born into a world that never intended to let you go," he said.

A strange, crawling sensation settled in my gut.

Vincent leaned forward, resting his forearms on the table.

"You were the daughter of a very powerful man."

I blinked. "What?"

He didn't repeat himself. He only watched, waiting for my mind to catch up.

I scoffed, shaking my head. "That's ridiculous."

"Is it?" His voice was too calm. "Then tell me—why are you here?"

I opened my mouth, but nothing came out.

"Why did you drop everything and come to France?" he continued. "Why do you speak a language you don't remember learning? Why do you dream of a dead man's name?" He tilted his head. "Why do you feel like you've been here before?"

A lump formed in my throat.

He was right.

He was too right.

Vincent sighed, leaning back slightly. "Your father was a feared man, Flower. He built an empire from nothing—one that thrived in the shadows, beyond the reach of law and order. He was powerful, ruthless, untouchable." A pause. "And you—" He hesitated, just for a second. "You were supposed to inherit it."

The words crashed over me like a tidal wave, but I barely had time to process them before he spoke again.

"But you weren't alone."

Something in his tone sent an eerie chill down my spine.

I frowned. "What do you mean?"

Vincent's gaze didn't waver.

"There were two of you."

A strange ringing filled my ears.

"Two," I echoed.

Vincent nodded once. "You and Astrid."

I stared at him.

My breath came short and sharp, a distant sound in the background of my mind. I felt weightless, detached from my own body.

Astrid.

The name I had spoken in the dark. The name that lingered at the edges of my dreams, like an old scar that refused to fade.

I had spent so long chasing his ghost.

And now—

"He was your twin, Lilith."

My pulse lurched.

Twin.

My throat tightened.

"That's not..." The words barely formed. "That's not possible."

Vincent didn't look away.

"It is," he said.

Something inside me twisted violently. I gripped the edge of the table, grounding myself, trying to breathe through the rising nausea.

If Astrid was my twin, then—

I swallowed hard. "Then why don't I remember him?"

Vincent's expression darkened.

"Because you were taken away."

The air left my lungs.

"Taken?" I whispered.

"By your mother."

The words hit me like a blade, slow and deep.

No.

No, that wasn't right. My mother...

Something cracked in my mind.

A memory, blurred and broken at the edges.

A cold hand gripping my wrist. A voice—low, filled with venom. "You are not his. You are mine."

My chest tightened.

Vincent kept talking, his voice steady, unraveling everything I thought I knew.

"She never wanted you to be part of your father's world."

My breathing grew uneven.

"Flower," Vincent said, quieter now. "Your mother... she wasn't a kind woman."

The words slid under my skin like splinters.

Vincent hesitated. But only for a second.

"She hurt you."

A sharp, phantom ache bloomed across my ribs.

My nails dug into my palms.

"She isolated you," Vincent continued. "Controlled you. Took away everything that tied you to—your name, your inheritance." He exhaled.

A shiver ran down my spine.

No.

That wasn't—

That wasn't true.

I got up without a word. That was ridiculous. I took a taxi all the way to my hotel without blinking. How?.. MY FATHER WAS A PART OF THE FRENCH UNDERWORLD?

NO WAIT.

I WAS...... FRENCH?

The sequence of events that took place after I arrived were crazy. I took a taxi.

The city blurred past the taxi window. Neon lights reflected off wet pavement, casting a distorted kaleidoscope of colors that pulsed with the beat of my racing heart. The streets of Paris—so foreign, so familiar—stretched out in a way that unsettled me.

The driver asked something in French, and I answered without hesitation.

The second the words left my mouth, my chest tightened.

I knew French.

Not in the way someone picks up phrases from movies or the way I took half-hearted German lessons in the institution I worked at. No. It was deeper, ingrained in my bones, slipping off my tongue like a second nature I had no memory of learning.

Vincent's words echoed in my skull.

"You will remember. And when you do—"

I shut my eyes, swallowing down the nausea that coiled in my stomach.

I didn't want to remember.

Yet something inside me stirred—a presence, an aching void that had been waiting for this moment.

I forced myself to breathe.

I would figure it out later.

The hotel lobby was nearly empty when I stepped inside, the soft hum of classical music playing through unseen speakers. The concierge greeted me in polite French, and I nodded absently, taking the key before retreating into the elevator.

The walls felt too close. The air is too thick.

By the time I reached my suite, my hands were shaking.

My fingers worked on autopilot, undoing the buttons of my coat, slipping off my shoes. My body moved through the motions as if rehearsed—like this was something I had done a hundred times before.

As always, I crept to the bathtub.

Less than halfway with boiling hot water.

I watched the steam rise against the mirror, fogging my reflection until it was nothing but a distorted blur.

Without hesitation, I stepped in.

The scalding temperature didn't make me flinch.

Didn't make me feel anything at all.

I exhaled, head tipping back against the porcelain, my eyes fluttering shut.

At some point, sleep took me.

And then—

A voice.

Soft. Low. Deliberate.

"Why do you like hot water, Isa?"

My breath hitched.

That name.

It coiled around me like a noose, suffocating, cloying. Not Lilith. Not a name I recognized, yet something deep inside me knew it.

A flicker of warmth—before the cold, crushing weight of memory swallowed it whole.

A sharp inhale.

Then my own voice, barely above a whisper.

"It's my coping mechanism."

The moment the words left my lips, the dream—no, the memory—rushed forward, pulling me under.

I was no longer in the bathtub.

I was small.

The walls were tall, looming, shadows stretching across the well decorated room. The air was thick, heavy with something acrid. My breath came in shallow gasps, my tiny hands clutching the fabric of a dress too large for me.

There was a woman.

Her face blurred at the edges, but her presence was suffocating.

I flinched as a sharp sting burned across my arm.

"Stop shouting."

The voice was calm, too calm.

Tears pricked at my eyes, but I refused to let them fall.

My skin burned, the scent of scorched flesh making my stomach lurch.

I wanted to pull away.

I wanted to scream.

I couldn't.

Another sharp sting.

My knees buckled. My tiny hands clenched into fists.

Then—

Darkness.

I could feel it—almost.

The water had gone lukewarm, but my skin still burned with pain. My hands trembled as I curled them into fists, pressing them against the cool floor to ground myself.

A bitter taste coated my tongue.

It wasn't just a dream.

It was a memory.

It had always been real.

My past wasn't just a void of forgotten years. It was a memory filled with horrors I had chosen to forget. And now—

Now, it was crawling its way back.

That lady burned me with hot water. At first, I screamed, sobbed until my throat was raw, and begged for it to stop. But it never did.

Days passed, and the pain clung to me like a second skin. The blisters, the aching sting, the way my flesh pulsed with each movement—it was unbearable. But then, something shifted. A realization.

Why run from it?

Why fear something that would always find me?

So I stopped.

Instead, I made myself immune.

I submerged myself in scalding water, let it consume me, let it strip away the weakness she despised. It hurt—God, it hurt—but at least this time, it was on my terms. I did it everyday so- so-

At least this time, when she burned me again,

I could muffle the eyes that die to well,

Quiet my hiccups with forceful will,

to show as if I fare well.

I woke up

I was in a state of dilemma, I wanted to know more, not out of curiosity but to validate how I didn't belong to this world. Not to anyone else but me because now even I knew one part of it was true but it just involved my mother so I couldn't tell if my father being in the mafia was true.

I took in my cloak and set out on the streets.

I wandered through the dimly lit streets of Paris, my thoughts tangled in a mess of half-formed memories and unanswered questions. The weight of Vincent's words still clung to me, suffocating and relentless. I pulled the coat tighter around her shoulders, the night's chill barely registering against her skin.

Then—I felt it.

A presence.

Someone was watching me.

I stopped walking. The streets weren't empty, but the figures passing by were nothing more than blurred shadows in the neon glow of the city. Yet, amidst the movement, one man stood still.

A stranger.

He was dressed in an unremarkable black coat, hands in his pockets, gaze locked onto me.

My pulse quickened.

He took a step forward.

Then another.

Before I could react, he closed the distance between them and, without a word, extended his hand. In his palm rested a phone—sleek, black, and unfamiliar.

I didn't move.

"It's for you," the man said, voice low, deliberate.

My fingers twitched. "Who—"

But before I could finish, the phone buzzed.

An unknown number.

A single word flashed across the screen.

Answer.

My breath caught.

I looked up—

The man was already gone.

I gave a lopsided smile, thinking it was from Vincent.

The phone vibrated again, insistent. A single, unrelenting buzz that seemed to echo in her chest.

My fingers hovered over the screen.

I swiped to accept.

For a moment, there was nothing. Just static. Then—

A song.

Soft, distant, barely above a whisper. A melody so familiar that her breath hitched. It curled around her like smoke, seeping into the cracks of her fractured mind, pulling at something deep, something buried—

My stomach twisted.

I knew this song.

I knew it the way I knew the feeling of blood on my hands, the way I knew the scent of burning flesh, the way I knew the echo of a scream that had long since faded.

The line crackled. Then, finally—

"Hello, Flower."

My throat closed.

The voice was smooth, calm, and laced with something chillingly familiar.

My grip on the phone tightened.

This wasn't possible.

Because the voice on the other end of the line—

It belonged to the man who sang to her in her dreams- no memories. Her hands clutched on the phone. Not in fear but in pure rage.

You're finally here. It pinged

I was in a state of confusion called Vincent because he was the only one she knew called her Flower.

"What kind of a prank was that, Vincent?" she scoffed.

"Same question, when did I prank you, flower"

"Then who- nothing," I halted as my gaze averted to the mobile in hand.

Curse words. An entire paragraph of it. He knew I hated them, from whatever my dreams- no memories showed me, because my mother used them to refer to me and I hated it to the deepest.

I half smiled. He surely knew how to get under my nerves, but not that it affected me. I mean, who could it even be?

The only people tied to my past are Vincent, my mother, and my dead brother... and who else? That was when my mind clicked back as memories rushed past my brain. It was... no, it had to be him, the man I saw most recently, the man I'd seen across the boardroom table, during that tense business meeting. His posture, the way he held himself, the subtle intensity in his gaze - it was undeniable. The man whose very existence was a mystery, a piece of a larger picture I was now to assemble, a connection to a past I was now ready to understand. He could be the same man.

NSSA- Flower, why are you so tense?
Is that wacko seriously following me? Yes he was saved as NSSA
What could it even mean- Not So Secret Admirer?

Me- 'cause you're not here :)

NSSA- You're the same as ever.

Me- I lost my memories mister, not my sense of self.

Looking more closely now, this man is kind of-. But who is he? Could I get more information from him? Maybe... But I need to know who he is first to get to him. Who is he even ?

My phone vibrated again. This time, it wasn't NSSA.

Vincent.

CHAPTER FOUR

SHOT AND ALIVE

I stared at the screen for a moment before answering.

"What now, Vincent?" I said, keeping my voice even.

His voice was as smooth as ever, but there was an edge to it this time. "Meet me."

I raised an eyebrow. "So soon? Miss me already?"

"I'm serious, Flower," he sighed. "There's more you need to know, and I'm done playing messenger through phone calls."

I leaned back in my chair, tapping my fingers against the table. "And where exactly do you propose we meet?"

He hesitated. Then, "The old clock tower. Midnight."

I frowned. "Really? A cliché meeting spot? What's next, fog rolling in and mysterious figures in the distance?"

His chuckle was brief, humorless. "Just be there, Lilith. Unless you'd rather stay in the dark."

The line went dead.

I stared at the screen, my reflection staring back at me. The old clock tower. I hadn't been there since—

I exhaled sharply, pushing the thought aside.

Fine. Midnight it is.

The clock tower loomed above, its silhouette carving through the night sky like a blade. I approached slowly, the sound of my boots against the worn pavement barely audible over the distant hum of the city.

Vincent stood against the railing, arms crossed, exuding the same effortless composure I remembered. If I remembered.

I didn't.

But something about him felt... familiar. A scent. A presence. A shadow in the corner of my mind that had always been there, waiting for me to turn around.

"You're late." His voice was even, but there was something beneath it. Amusement? Annoyance? Something else entirely?

I tilted my head. "You gave me a whole five hours' notice. Be grateful I showed up."

A smirk flickered at the edge of his lips. "Same sharp tongue." He paused, eyes scanning my face. "But you don't remember, do you?"

I forced a shrug. "That's the whole issue, isn't it?"

He exhaled, looking down at the city below. "Then let me remind you." His voice was quieter now. "Who you were. What you were."

I folded my arms, mirroring his stance. "Go on, enlighten me."

He studied me for a moment, his gaze flickering with something unreadable. Then, finally, he spoke.

"You were reckless." A statement, not an insult. "Unhinged, even."

A dry laugh escaped me. "Sounds charming."

"It was terrifying."

I smiled.

Then—

A sharp, searing pain tore through my arm, hot and sudden, like fire bursting beneath my skin.

The world slowed.

For a moment, I didn't fully register what had happened. Just the sting, the wet warmth spreading down my sleeve, the way my breath hitched in my throat.

Then, the delayed crack of a gunshot rang through the air.

I stumbled back, my hand flying to my bicep. Blood. Sticky, warm, seeping through my fingers. The fabric of my coat darkened fast, clinging to my skin as the pain finally caught up to me—sharp, pulsing, alive.

Vincent moved before I did.

His body tensed, his eyes snapping toward the darkness beyond the streetlights. I barely had time to glance up before another shot rang out.

This one—I saw.

The flash of the muzzle, the trajectory of the bullet slicing through the air.

Instinct took over.

I shoved Vincent back.

"Move!"

The bullet missed him.

Vincent's hands were on me before I could steady myself, gripping my uninjured arm, pulling me upright. His touch was rough, firm. I could hear his breath—too controlled, too even—but beneath that calm was something else.

Panic.

"You're hit." His voice was low, taut.

I sucked in a sharp breath through my teeth. "Noticed that."

My coat was damp, the warm, metallic scent of my own blood thick in the air. My arm throbbed, but I forced my focus past the pain.

The shooter was still there.

Not running.

Just watching.

Vincent followed my gaze. His fingers twitched where they still clutched me, his stance shifting ever so slightly. Protective. Ready.

"They're not in a hurry," I muttered. My voice was steady, but my body disagreed—my arm pulsed, my blood smeared across my own fingers as I pulled my hand away from the wound.

Vincent's jaw clenched. "Because they wanted to hit you."

"Well, mission accomplished," I bit back, pressing my palm harder against my arm. The pain sharpened. Good. It kept me grounded.

Another slow movement from the shadows. A tilt of the head. The shooter's posture remained the same—casual, unconcerned. Like they were waiting for something.

Waiting for me to react.

Vincent tugged at me. "We need to move."

I hesitated for half a second too long.

My vision blurred, just for a fraction of a second—just enough for Vincent to pull me. His arm wrapped around my waist, half-guiding, half-dragging me away from the open street.

I hissed at the pressure on my arm. "I can walk."

"You're bleeding," he shot back, his grip unwavering.

I forced my legs to move. Blood dripped from my fingers, staining the pavement in a trail behind me. The city lights blurred, the alley spinning as adrenaline warred with the pain.

The shooter didn't follow.

Didn't need to.

They had made their point.

But next time, they wouldn't get the chance to walk away.

I barely made it to the bathroom before my legs gave out. My knees hit the tile, hard, but the pain barely registered over the searing heat in my arm.

My breath came in short, ragged bursts. I peeled my coat off, my fingers slick with blood. It stuck to my skin, warm and wet, seeping through the fabric of my sleeve in thick, crimson patches.

I needed to move.

I forced myself upright, gripping the counter for balance. The bathroom light was too bright, making my reflection sharp, almost unnatural. My own face stared back at me—pale, blood-splattered, eyes blown wide with pain and adrenaline.

The wound on my arm wasn't going to kill me. But the bullet was still inside.

A sharp breath left my lips. My fingers trembled as I reached under the sink, yanking out the first aid kit. It clattered onto the counter.

I pulled out what I needed—gauze, antiseptic, a pair of tweezers. But I knew tweezers weren't going to cut it.

I needed something sharper.

My hand found the switchblade in my pocket. I flicked it open with a practiced snap. The blade gleamed under the fluorescent light, clean and sharp.

I swallowed hard.

Then, without hesitating, I pressed the tip of the knife against the raw, pulsing wound.

Pain flared, white-hot and immediate. My vision darkened at the edges, my breath hitching in my throat. I clenched my jaw so tightly I thought my teeth might crack.

The first cut was shallow. Testing. My stomach clenched, bile rising in my throat, but I forced the blade deeper.

I had to do this.

The pain was unbearable, blinding. Every nerve screamed in protest as I dug the blade in, parting flesh, making the wound gape wider. Blood welled up, thick and dark, spilling over my fingers.

My breathing came in short, sharp gasps.

Almost there.

The tip of the knife scraped something solid. A sharp, foreign pressure buried deep in muscle.

I exhaled through clenched teeth.

I dropped the knife into the sink with a clatter, my bloodied fingers scrambling for the tweezers. My hands were shaking too much.

"Come on," I muttered, voice barely above a whisper.

I shoved the metal tips into the wound, feeling around for the bullet. My vision swam. My body trembled violently, every nerve alight with agony.

There.

I gritted my teeth and clamped down on the slick, unyielding metal.

The moment I pulled, the world narrowed to nothing but pain.

It felt like my body was ripping apart from the inside, like fire and steel and pure, raw agony all at once. A strangled sound tore from my throat—something between a sob and a growl.

The bullet slid free with a sickening, wet sound.

I nearly collapsed.

Blood gushed from the wound, spilling down my arm in thick, sluggish waves. My arms felt too heavy, my fingers numb as I dropped the bullet onto the counter. It clinked against the porcelain—small, harmless-looking, but I had never hated anything more.

I forced myself to move.

Grabbing the antiseptic, I poured it straight into the wound.

Pain.

I bit down on my lip so hard I tasted copper, my body convulsing as fire licked through my veins. My breath came in sharp, shallow gasps, spots dancing at the edges of my vision.

I was going to pass out.

No.

I grabbed the needle. My fingers were slick with blood, shaking so badly I could barely thread it, but I did.

The first stitch sent a fresh wave of nausea crashing over me.

One down.

The second was worse.

By the time I reached the last, I was shaking uncontrollably, my skin clammy, my breath coming in uneven, ragged bursts. I tied the knot off with bloody, unsteady fingers, pressing a bandage over the wound.

I didn't move for a long moment.

Just breathed.

Then, slowly, I dragged myself upright, gripping the counter for balance. My body screamed in protest, my vision still swimming. But I was done.

I was alive.

And now, I was going to find whoever did this.

And make them wish they had finished the job.

I looked at the blood in my hands.

This bullet felt known.

The pain it gave me was known.

It wasn't like knowing a movie by heart, but recalling flashes of bloopers without the full plot, It wasn't the song's chorus but its beat, what I remembered was not my life's entire story but only a few flashes like a sense of deja vu that loaded back when Vincent's few word from the description matched to those flashes .

It wasn't like remembering—no, it was like rediscovering. And each fragment that surfaced felt like a wound reopening, bleeding, and rediscovering pain, no idea of what.

I hate my life.

I am no poet.

Never have I written poetry, Neither is this poetry, I sometimes think on those lines , but- but today I even discovered this part of me... I smiled through that agony.

Sometimes I think if I could-

Halt this book.

Freeze this scene.

Pause This song.

Just for a moment—long enough to step away, to exist outside of it.

Not to end it, not to erase it, just to slip beyond its grasp.

I don't want to die.

I don't want to break.

I just need a little rest.

To close my eyes without the weight of yesterday pressing down on my chest.

To breathe without feeling like every inhale is borrowed time.

To exist—not as a survivor, not as a fighter, not as a puzzle missing too many pieces—

But simply as myself.

I want silence, not oblivion.

Stillness, not emptiness.

Just a brief moment where the past does not reach for me,

Where memories do not claw their way back.

Just a little rest.

Then—I'll press play again.

"Who am I, Vincent"

I didn't let him answer not yet.

"Appoint me a man"

"Sure"

"Someone trustworthy... at the earliest"

Yes, I didn't ask Vincent to leave instead he drove me here.

I could not visit the hospitals because this was a gunshot we were talking about.

This apartment was of Eve's relatives' old apartment I guess.

I sat on the couch across the room and gave it a thought.

I was here for answers.

Then why do I get more Questions than conclusions?

NSSA- Are you fine, Flower? That was not meant for you, but it stopped you at least.

Me-Stop me?

NSSA- Why are you so desperate, Flower? If I would have killed him would you have liked my gift?

Me- Yeah! Maybe I would've reciprocated it.

I just shut the phone.

Desperate?

Well, anyone would be desperate if they were unknown. If they were forced to live in the dark while someone else faceless held the light just out of reach.

I stared at the phone, the screen still dimly glowing. My fingers curled around it, gripping tighter, as if I could squeeze answers out of cold glass and metal.

It wasn't just the words. It was the way they crawled under my skin, wrapping around my bones like an old, forgotten ghost. A presence that was both distant and intimate. He knew me. More than I knew myself.

I exhaled, steadying my breath. Reciprocate? Maybe I would.

Maybe I'd turn this game around.

Maybe it was time to stop waiting for answers and start pulling them out myself.

SLIPPING INTO DEEP SLEEP

I tapped my fingers against the phone, the rhythm slow, deliberate. A game. That's what this was, wasn't it? He was toying with me, dangling breadcrumbs just close enough to keep me moving but never close enough to satisfy my hunger for the truth.

I wasn't going to be led around like a clueless pawn.

Not anymore.

I opened my messages again.

Me- You like control, don't you?

Me- Watching from a distance, leaving little gifts, saying just enough to make sure I stay curious.

Me- But I wonder... how would you feel if the roles were reversed?

Seconds passed. Then a minute. No reply.

I smirked. Good.

Grabbing my coat, I slid my knife into my pocket and stepped out onto the dimly lit streets. If he wouldn't hand me the answers, I'd take them myself.

And I knew just where to start.

My destination was clear—Vincent. He knew more than he let on. He always did. And if anyone could point me in the right direction, it was him.

I couldn't contact him right now. He was already too weak and retired to his bungalow at dawn.

A few days went by as I worked from home. Yes, I am a corporate slave. I need meals to survive.

I had asked him when he was free. I decided to meet him.

The night air was crisp, slicing through my skin like a blade. The city pulsed around me—horns blaring, voices overlapping, neon lights flickering like dying stars. I navigated through it all with ease, the path etched into my mind as if I'd walked it a thousand times before.

By the time I reached Vincent's place, the air was thick with something unseen. A tension. A weight pressing down on my ribs.

I knocked.

No answer.

I knocked again, harder this time.

Still nothing.

A sinking feeling coiled in my stomach. I tried the door. Unlocked.

That wasn't right. Vincent was paranoid. Always triple-checking locks, always making sure he was one step ahead of anyone who might want to silence him.

I pushed inside.

The scent of iron hit me first.

Then the sight followed.

Vincent. Slumped against the wall, blood pooling beneath him, painting the floor a deep, sickening crimson.

My breath caught. I dropped to my knees beside him, my hands hovering over his wounds. Multiple gunshots. A professional job—clean shots, but not clean enough. He was still breathing, barely.

He was shot again.

His eyes flickered open, unfocused at first, then locking onto mine. He tried to speak, but all that came out was a rasping sound.

"Don't talk," I muttered, ripping off a piece of my sleeve to press against one of the wounds. "Just stay with me."

He let out a strained chuckle, wincing. "You... always were... stubborn."

I ignored him, my hands moving fast, applying pressure, trying to slow the bleeding. "Who did this?"

Vincent coughed, blood speckling his lips. "The same."

My blood ran cold.

This wasn't a game anymore.

The room felt smaller, the walls closing in as Vincent's words settled deep in my chest, cold and sharp.

A chill ran down my spine, but I forced it down, focused on the task at hand. Vincent was losing too much blood. His breaths were shallow, his pulse weak. I had to work fast.

Three shots. One to the shoulder, one on his ribs, and the last—my stomach twisted—it had lodged itself deep in his abdomen.

"Who—whoever did this," Vincent wheezed, his voice laced with pain, "they knew what they were doing... didn't aim to kill me immediately."

No, they hadn't. They wanted him to suffer.

I pressed my hands against his wounds, feeling the hot, sticky blood seep between my fingers. He groaned but didn't push me away.

"This is going to hurt."

A humorless smirk tugged at his lips. "Everything... already hurts."

I ignored him and reached for my knife.

A tremor ran through him. "Lilith..."

I didn't answer. With one swift motion, I sterilized the blade with a lighter, the flame flickering unsteadily between us.

His breathing hitched. "You're not a doctor."

"I never said I was."

With steady hands, I dug into the wound. His body convulsed, a strangled groan tearing from his throat. The bullet was deep, but I had no choice—I couldn't risk waiting for help. The moment I'd stepped into this room, I knew we were alone. Whoever shot him made sure of that.

Vincent's fingers dug into the floor as he fought against the pain, but he didn't scream.

"I'll get it out," I muttered, my voice more for myself than for him. "I have to."

Minutes stretched into eternity. My hands were slick with his blood by the time I finally fished out the bullet. I tossed it aside, immediately pressing my torn sleeve against the open wound.

His chest rose and fell in erratic gasps. He was still losing blood, but—

He was alive.

That had to be enough.

For now.

I exhaled sharply, my mind already racing to the next step. NSSA—whoever the hell he really was?

I'd played along with his game for too long.

Now, I am going to end it.

And this time?

I wouldn't miss it.

I huffed, my patience thinning with every passing second. Blood soaked through his clothes, my hands, the floor—everywhere. It was a mess, a gruesome, disgusting mess.

And Vincent, the idiot bleeding out beneath me, had the audacity to smirk.

"You look mad, Flower." His voice was hoarse, barely above a whisper.

I was mad. Furious, even. Livid.

"Mad? Oh, Vincent, I am beyond mad," I snapped, adjusting the pressure on his wound. He sucked in a sharp breath. Good. "You were in the mafia, Vincent. A trained, seasoned, supposedly competent criminal. And yet, here you are, lying in a pool of your own blood because you got shot almost—twice."

I scoffed, shaking my head as I worked. "Unbelievable. Honestly. What kind of mafia man gets shot twice? Once, okay. Maybe you were caught off guard. But twice?"

"Must be losing my touch," he murmured.

"Oh, must be," I mocked, grabbing the torn fabric of his shirt and pressing it harder against the wound. He groaned, his head tilting back against the cold ground. "Who even shot you, Vincent? What did you even do, knock on the wrong door?"

He let out a strained chuckle. "Something like that."

I rolled my eyes, muttering under my breath as I yanked open my bag. No proper medical supplies. Of course not. Why would I? It's not like I planned on playing trauma surgeon tonight.

I dug out a pocket knife, the blade glinting under the dim lighting of the room. "Alright, genius. We need to stop the bleeding."

Vincent's eyes flickered to the knife, then back to me. "What exactly... are you planning to do with that?"

I gave him a dry look. "What do you think? You're bleeding out,dumbo . Unless you'd rather die dramatically in my arms."

He opened his mouth—probably to say something smug—but I didn't give him the chance. Instead, I tore a strip of fabric from my own shirt, using it to tie off one of the wounds as tightly as I could. His entire body tensed beneath my hands.

"God, Vincent, you're a real eyesore ," I muttered, shifting my focus to his second wound. It was worse. Bloodier. Too deep.

He smirked weakly. "Not the first time you've said that."

I shot him a glare. "Not the first time you deserved it either."

He chuckled—then immediately winced, his body jerking from the pain. I swallowed hard. He was getting weaker. I needed to work faster.

"Just—hold on," I muttered, positioning the blade against his wound. "This is going to hurt."

He exhaled through gritted teeth. "Already does."

"Yeah, well—" I pressed down, cutting away the excess bloodied fabric—"it's about to get a lot worse."

His muffled groan told me I was right.

Vincent's body tensed beneath my hands, every muscle rigid with pain. His breath came in sharp, shallow gasps, and for a moment, I wondered if he was even conscious enough to withstand what I was about to do.

Too bad. He didn't have a choice.

I wiped the blade clean on what remained of his ruined shirt. The metal gleamed under the flickering streetlight, cruel and merciless, just like the night itself.

"You still with me, Vincent?" I asked, more for my own reassurance than his.

His eyelids fluttered, and he let out a strangled breath. "Unfortunately."

I smirked despite the situation. "Good. Because this is going to be hell."

He barely had time to process before I pressed the blade to his wound, digging just deep enough to clear away the debris.

Vincent's entire body arched off the ground, a strangled growl tearing from his throat. His fingers clawed at the pavement, nails scraping against stone as he struggled against the pain.

"Stay still," I ordered, pressing down harder on his shoulder to pin him in place.

He panted, his forehead slick with sweat. "You're—insane."

"Says the man who got shot two times in one fortnight ," I shot back.

His head lolled to the side, exhaustion finally starting to creep in.

I was running out of time.

I clenched my jaw. "You're not dying on me, Vincent. You hear me?"

His lips twitched. "Wouldn't dream of it, Flower."

I exhaled sharply, finishing the last of the bandaging before pressing my palm against his uninjured side. "We need to move. You can't stay here."

His eyes flickered open just enough to meet mine. "Can't exactly walk, sweetheart."

I rolled my eyes. "Then I guess I'm dragging your dead body out of here."

Vincent let out a weak chuckle, but I didn't miss the way his fingers twitched—reaching for something, someone.

And for reasons I couldn't quite understand, I grabbed his hand and held on.

I didn't quite know him but one thing was sure, he had to be my family or friend or someone I cherished, he was my brother after all.

I will take him to the doctor I searched for.

"I said- no hospitals"

"You know what Vincent, if you really want to die, Trust me I have more creative ways, at least make it to the headlines, dude"

"You tryna kill me Flower?"

"Wish I could"

I had searched for a hospital doctor, he could treat him, I did the first aid though.

He won't leak the patient's personal info.

I get a wave of flashes every day now, as soon as I spot blood.

The moment the crimson pools, my vision fractures. I'm not here anymore.

I'm back in that dimly lit corridor, the air thick with the metallic stench. Footsteps echo. My hands tremble as I reach out—only to feel the warmth of something slick and wet. His body, crumpled, lifeless.

Then—another snap. The scene shifts. I see her. Evelyn. Standing there, shadowed, indifferent. The weight in her hand glints under the dim glow. My chest tightens, fury and anguish colliding.

Something cracks inside me. The world tilts. The memories press in too fast, too hard—suffocating.

My knees buckle. I barely feel myself hit the ground. Darkness rushes up like a tidal wave, swallowing me whole.

Then—nothing.

No pain. No sound. No light. Just an endless void.

Somewhere, far away, voices call my name. But I can't answer. I can't move.

I'm trapped.

CHAPTER SIX

MEMORIES.

The doctors came rushing in when they saw my eyes flutter open.

"We need to find who killed Astrid... Maybe he's after us," he continued saying to the man... Leo.

"Maybe he knows that you've returned , that's why he plans to kill us."

He saw me moving.

"Lilith, you are fine right?" Vincent asked, pressing down on my hands.

"Yeah, I am better just a bit.."

Yeah. Exhausted as I always have been. But now it's time to act upon it. I surely have to get out of this loop.

"Vincent I need to talk to you"

"At my place. Tomorrow at 1PM. Okay?"

"But-"

"I am getting out of this cramped place ,today– How long was I out for?"

"5"

Oh so 5 hours.

"5 weeks"

Wow. That's a lot.

"I've rested a lot"

He didn't protest.

I informed Aaron. I am resigning, I was working on a business model for the past two years, I needed something to rely on. The company had its set of lows, but now it made just enough for my expenses, I didn't want anything else. My memories itself are a luxury.

I returned back and sat on the couch looking at my phone's screen.

The room resonated with a ringing. It was the bell. He came to reveal truths only few knew.

"Sit"

"We're safe, speak"

He spoke as my heart thumped.

"Call me by my name"

"Lilith?"

"No"

"Isadora"

"Better …"

"Astrid died, Isadora, in your hands. Someone killed him but we don't know who. We sent you away to—Evelyn. I knew you'll come back one day. I just didn't know when. You were young, just twenty three. I knew you could make it in life out of this world.

I have searched for who killed him but no record whatsoever."

"Continue speaking"

"As I told you, your father- Rapael Francis Lemaire was a part of the best mafias across the globe. He married your mother at an early age. You were born with Astrid, but after their divorce, she took you"

"She treated you horribly, you didn't have a name even, we gave you a name though 'Isadora Francis Lemaire' "

"Then, you?"

"I am your step brother," he paused then "We took you with ourselves when your mother died"

"That's enough for now"

"Remember we're in this together whatever happens. We will get to who killed Astrid, Vincent."

He gave me a quick nod before leaving.

I too got up and set out on the streets without anything warm.

The wind bit through my clothes, sharp against my skin, but I welcomed it.

I strolled without any thoughts. Just silence. Just the dull throb in my arm, and the even duller throb in my chest.

The city buzzed faintly around me—cars, lights, lives. I walked like a ghost slipping through it all. Somewhere between Lilith and Isadora. Somewhere between who I was and who I had no choice but to become again.

By the time I reached home, my fingers were numb.

The door gave way with a slow creak, groaning like it resented being opened.

Darkness pooled inside the apartment.

I hadn't left the lights on, but something in the air felt... wrong.

Not loud wrong—quiet wrong. The kind of silence that presses against your chest and listens too closely.

I stepped in. The door clicked shut behind me like a gavel.

The air hung heavy, stagnant. Breathing felt like sipping static.

Still, sleep is called louder than instinct. I was too drained to care.

I moved on autopilot toward the bedroom, muscles aching, eyelids weighted.

Something slick shifted beneath my foot—warm, wet and slimy.

But I didn't stop.

Didn't look.

Didn't care.

I just wanted to sleep. Let the darkness have the apartment tonight—so long as it left my dreams alone.

I woke up to a rotten smell and buzzing of houseflies.

I looked down there at the centre of a pool of blood lied a woman.. No man, its face distorted and crushed by hitting against it. I moved closer.

I took hold of my Springfield Echelon.

I looked at his face lolled at one side. His wounds made him unrecognisable, taking the tip of my pistol I placed it at the right of his chin and turned him.

It was him .

The representative from the other company that day.

Now, his eyes stared blankly at the ceiling, mouth slightly parted like he had died mid-sentence.

I stepped back, lowering the gun.

What the hell was he doing here?

And why him, of all people?

My mind raced. There were no signs of forced entry, no overturned furniture. He hadn't fought back. Or maybe he hadn't gotten the chance. But someone had wanted me to find him like this. Someone had chosen my room for this... message.

Because that's what this was. Not just a death. A warning.

My gaze dropped to the floor where something glinted near his body.

I crouched carefully and picked it up.

My breath hitched.

Suddenly the room felt tighter, the shadows longer, as if they were watching, listening. I stood quickly, heart thudding in my ears. The silence was too complete.

I needed to get out.

I grabbed my coat and phone, taking one last look at the body before stepping outside. The streetlight flickered overhead. Somewhere in the distance, a siren wailed.

I didn't inform the police.

Not yet.

Not until I knew who I was really fighting.

And what they still remembered about Isadora Francis Lemaire.

I let out a sigh but not before calling Leo.

"There's a dead body." I sighed yet again.

"Where?"

"At my place. Get it, dispose it off, after taking a few samples."

"Okay"

He agrees to almost everything without a question. He is my right hand man for now. Aaron fake bowled when I told this to him.

Maybe he was scared he'd lose his job.

I looked at his portfolio. Nothing doubtful other than his gestures.

I retired back after two hours and sat in the tub with hot water. My wound stings, obviously! So, I let it sting. It reminds me constantly of the goal in mind.

What's with this pin?

I thought while the pin remained in the plastic ziplock.

The pin was stained in blood. I kept it aside on the stand.

I got outside and took in hand a notepad and pen and started taking notes.

I paused and looked at it, with a sense of realisation that took over me when my gaze saw the name 'NSSA'. Half of the mysteries will reveal themselves when we find him.

I need to find him on my own.

I expected him to be this company representative but no he was dead. So who?

Perhaps someone I didn't know. Not at all or maybe partly.

I received a message on that phone again

[Unknown Number]-You looked tired tonight.

Isadora-Who is this?

[Unknown Number]-Names are fluid, aren't they? But let's just say I've always been near.

Isadora-Are you that freak ?NSSA?

[Unknown Number-I've been called worse.

But yes. For now.

Isadora-What do you want?

-

To see how much of Isadora is still intact.

To see if the wound still stings.

Isadora-Where were you the night Astrid died?

NSSA-Straight to the point?

Let's see...

Closer than you think.

Far enough to survive.

Isadora-Why now? Why reach out after all these years?

NSSA-Because now you're asking the right questions.
Because you're finally ready to remember.

Isadora-Meet me.

NSSA-We already have.

I could tell one thing for sure, that NSSA was far more close and acquainted with who I was. It was me who was in the dark , but not for long.

I could trust no one. I called Aaron to replace him with Leo, obviously.

He agreed.

I really needed to know who NSSA was and what his motive was. It was really confusing.

He messaged me something again

My phone buzzed again.

NSSA-Still think this is a game, Isadora?

There was an image attached.

I hesitated—because something inside me already knew it wasn't just another threat.

I tapped the photo open.

A pair of hands. Pale. Severed clean at the wrist. Resting on a velvet cloth.

Nails painted a familiar shade of plum.

On the ring finger—a silver band. Evelyn's.

I had seen it enough times to remember its engraving:

"No mercy, no madness."

I palmed my forehead before running my fingers through my hair.

I kept the phone, but the image stayed burned behind my eyes.

Another message appeared.

NSSA- You think replacing your shadows will change anything? You're playing the game now, Isa. And players don't get to leave.

I stared at the message, the photo lying in my mind like a landmine.

Was she dead?

Was this... old?

Was this even real?

Or just a sick way of reminding me that NSSA knew where to hurt—and exactly how deep.

I called Leo.

No answer.

I called Evelyn.

Straight to voicemail.

Everything around me started to constrict—walls, breath, logic.

And that's when I noticed it—on the velvet beneath the hands in the photo.

A cufflink.

With "Theodore".

Anyway, what about Evelyn? Whose side was he really on?

I don't even know anymore.

I looked at message from leo and kept my phone down then picked it up again, widening my eyes, "The thing you got, you should send it to the forensics"

I never told him about this. Wait. Was I correct?

A few days later-*

I was at my apartment, Evelyn hadn't replied and I was so done with these mind games.

I didn't move.

My breath slowed, but not from calm. More like being held under water—where stillness wasn't peace, but survival.

NSSA—Tell Aaron I said hello.

It couldn't mean what it sounded like. It was taunting. Just another one of NSSA's riddles. A bluff meant to unravel me. I clenched my jaw and leaned over the tub's edge, retrieving the phone. It had gone black, but the message remained, like a scar burned into glass.

I deleted it. For now.

When I stepped out, Aaron was making coffee, his sleeves rolled up, the same easy posture he always carried. Safe. Reliable.

He was staying on the floor above mine, but knew my passcode, for security reasons.

"Didn't hear you get up," I murmured, watching him.

He smiled over his shoulder. "Didn't want to wake you. Figured you needed rest."

I did.

"You ever get the feeling someone's playing chess with your life?" I asked, sitting at the counter.

He poured two mugs. "Every day. But I play better."

I forced a laugh. He always knew how to ground me—too well. Sometimes, I wondered if that was the problem. Still, I reached for the mug, letting my fingers brush his as I took it.

"Thanks," I said softly.

"Always," he replied.

Later that night, I tucked the bloodied pin back into its ziplock and slid it into the baseboard behind the mirror—one of the only hiding places I hadn't already compromised. I didn't know what else to do.

The next morning, I found him already suited up, tie loose around his collar, flipping through one of my red-inked files.

"You sleep?" he asked.

"Like a corpse."

He glanced up. "Comforting."

I nodded toward the folder. "Find anything interesting?"

He closed it and handed it back. "Just lines on paper until we've got someone to question. Leo?"

"No response yet. He's gone quiet."

Aaron hesitated. "Want me to look into it?"

I did. But I said, "Not yet. Give him time."

Because if Leo was really in trouble, I'd have blood on my hands. And if he wasn't—if he was NSSA? Then he was trying to beat me at my own game.

But Aaron...

Aaron had stayed. Even through all of it. I remembered the night... maybe ... after when I got the first dream about deaths, when I hadn't eaten in two days and everything felt like it was collapsing from the inside. Aaron had carried me to the couch, wrapped me in his coat, and sat with me until dawn. He hadn't spoken. Just stayed.

No spy would do that.

Right?

Later that day, I received another message from him.

NSSA: I liked your choice of words. "Corpse." You're closer to the truth than you think.

I stared at the screen. Every sentence felt like a key to a locked door in my past. And each key brought me closer to the room I didn't want to open.

I sat next to Aaron.

"Talk to me, my brain's a mess"

"Okay what do you need to know"

"Mine name's Isadora Francis Lemaire"

"I know"

"Who were you"

"Evelyn's brother, she was your... no more than... acquaintance "

I needed space.

The walls of the apartment felt too loud, too knowing. I couldn't breathe in the silence anymore, not without feeling like someone—or something—was watching.

I told Aaron I'd be out. Left without saying where. Just grabbed my coat, phone, and keys and slipped into the night.

I walked three blocks, past shuttered windows and flickering streetlamps, until I reached the old bookstore on the corner. The one with no working cameras. The one with a bell above the door that never rang, no matter how many times you walked through.

Inside, the scent hit me first. Yellowed paper, old wood, dust, and something faintly sweet—maybe dried lavender or forgotten ink. I wandered the aisles slowly, fingers grazing the brittle spines of forgotten stories.

I picked a novel at random. One with a cracked spine and no title left on the cover. Paid in cash. No receipt. Then tucked myself into the farthest booth in the back, a dim corner where no one ever looked.

That's when I noticed the book.

Not the one I bought.

The one tucked behind it on the shelf, half-concealed like it didn't want to be found.

Its spine was cracked, the cover worn to soft leather. The title, barely legible under a layer of time:

"Names of God."

CHAPTER SEVEN

"NAMES OF GOD"

I don't know what made me take it. Instinct, maybe. Or fate. I opened the cover slowly, my breath shallow.

Inside, on the front page, a single name was scribbled in blocky, unmistakable handwriting.

I flipped through the pages, scanning without reading—until I saw it.

"ISADORA – GIFT OF ISIS."

My name. My meaning.

I knew that. Always had. But seeing it here, in this strange old book I wasn't meant to find, made something twist behind my ribs.

I turned a few more pages. The paper felt fragile, like it might crumble if I moved too fast.

Then I saw it.

A word. A name. Circled in red.

"EO – GIFT OF GOD."

But faded.

My breath caught. The ink looked fresh, though the page didn't. Right below the name, in fine slanted handwriting, someone had scribbled:

"Not forgotten. Just rewritten."

I stared at the words until they blurred. My heartbeat pulsed at my throat, faster, louder.

I fumbled for my phone and called Vincent.

He answered almost immediately. "Isadora?"

"Meet me," I said, voice tight. "Not at my apartment."

A pause. Then, "Okay. Be at my place?"

I shook my head before realizing he couldn't see me. "No. Café in front of your place."

Another beat. "I'll be there."

I didn't wait to respond. I was already moving.

I reached his building in record time, practically speed-walking through the dark with the book clutched tight beneath my coat.

The café lights glowed amber against the frost-glazed windows. I could see him already—Vincent—sitting in the corner by the window.

Vincent looked up the moment I entered, eyes narrowing, concern immediately etching into the lines of his face.

I didn't speak at first. Just slid into the booth across from him and set the book down between us like evidence on a table. His gaze dropped to it.

"'Names of God'?" he read aloud, then glanced back up. "Where did you find this?"

"Bookstore near 3rd and Haven," I murmured. "It wasn't on display. It was... tucked behind another one. Like someone wanted it to be found, but only by the right hands."

He didn't touch it. "You opened it?"

I nodded. "Page by page."

"And?" His voice was soft, but not casual. It was the kind of softness that meant danger—like a trap just shy of snapping.

I opened the book again, turned to the first page, and tapped where the name was scrawled in blocky, childlike handwriting.

"eo."

Vincent blinked slowly. "Leo?," he echoed. But I saw it—the flicker in his expression. A memory surfacing. He knew.

I flipped a few more pages. "My name's in here too. Isadora—'Gift of Isis.'" I met his eyes. "I know the meaning. That's not what rattled me. What rattled me was the way it's written. It's personal. Not academic. Not a dictionary of names. Like someone was keeping... track. Watching."

His jaw tightened. "And the other one?...eo...?"

I tapped again. "Circled. Red ink. Fresh."

Vincent finally reached out and turned a page. He skimmed the handwriting. "This isn't just some dusty old relic, Isa."

"No," I said. "It's a message."

We sat in silence. Outside, the wind pressed faintly against the glass, the city's noise muffled beneath the quiet hum of the heater above us.

I pulled out the photograph. "This was inside."

Vincent's eyes scanned it—and then froze. "Astrid," he breathed.

I nodded. "And the boy beside him."

His hands clenched. "Where did you say you found this again?"

"I didn't. It found me."

He looked like he was holding something back. I could see it building behind his eyes—panic, recognition, denial.

"I need you to tell me everything you know about Leo," I said firmly.

His mouth opened, then closed. He leaned back, exhaling slowly. "His name doesn't mean Gift of God."

"I know. But he wants to be my shadow, be it a genuine or a forced one, he wants our name to correspond."

Vincent leaned forward. "If it's him... if it's really Leo...you can't trust anything anymore. Not names. Not faces. Not even—"

"I know," I said sharply, cutting him off. "But that's not the worst part."

He frowned. "What is?"

I met his gaze, voice low. "The initials."

He blinked.

"NSSA," I said. "They've been hounding me for months. Always a step ahead. Always knowing exactly what to say, how to hurt." I paused, letting it sink in. "I never knew what it stood for. But now I think I do."

Vincent stared.

I slid the book toward him, whispering, "Not just a codename. Not just a threat."

He tilted his head, reading again.

I gave him a confused look.

He looked up at me, waiting.

NSSA.

"Not Someone. Someone Specific." My voice was shaking now.

"Who's that?"

"He knows too much."

"Could Leo be this person?"

He didn't flinch.

"Speak up," I said, almost about to point my gun at him. No, what was I thinking?

Vincent let out a slow, horrified breath.

Vincent's hands were white-knuckled around the mug. "Isa, if that's true..."

The room fell into a thick silence.

"You can't trust anyone, not even Leo."

After a long moment, Vincent spoke, voice grave. "You told Aaron?"

I shook my head. "Not yet. He's been... I don't know. He's too close to this. And he's the only thing that's felt stable."

"You trust him?"

"With my life," I said without hesitation. "But not with this. Not yet."

Vincent didn't argue. He just nodded, the weight of the revelation settling between us.

The book sat on the table, its cover dark and unassuming. But inside, it held a legacy I hadn't consented to inherit.

I leaned back in my seat, suddenly exhausted.

"I thought I'd buried Isadora Francis Lemaire a long time ago," I said quietly. Rethinking how I almost pointed my gun at him for answers.

Vincent watched me. "Looks like she just got dug back up."

I shot a glare at him.

The apartment was dark when I returned.

Not empty—just quiet. The kind of quiet that presses too close, like something holding its breath.

I locked the door behind me and slid off my coat, the book still tucked under one arm. I'd wrapped it in brown paper at the last minute—something about walking in with a book titled Names of God felt like tempting fate.

Aaron appeared from the hallway.

He smiled when he saw me, but the expression faltered just slightly. "You were gone a while."

"Got caught in the rain," I lied. "Bookstore ran late."

He crossed the room and gently took the paper-wrapped package from my hands. "You okay?"

I nodded, too quickly.

He didn't press. Just reached out and flicked my head.

"What the he-"

"Shut up, you annoy me, why so serious? Chill, you should rest at home." He said, guiding me to the table.

"Come sit," he said softly. "I made Chamomile tea."

"What, I don't have digestive issues."

"I know. What could I do, that's the only thing you had in the fridge."

I followed him into the kitchen, grateful for the warmth. The kettle still whistled faintly. He poured the tea, added honey like he always did for me, and set the mug down in front of my seat.

Everything he did was careful. Thoughtful. Measured.

Safe.

"You sure everything's okay?" he asked again.

I stared into the tea.

"I remembered something today," I said slowly. "About the past. About Astrid."

Aaron leaned on the counter across from me, eyes alert but patient. "What kind of memory?"

"Someone he used to know," I murmured. "From before."

Aaron nodded for me to continue.

I didn't.

Because I couldn't tell him yet. Not about EO. Not about the initials. Not about the look on Vincent's face when he realized this wasn't just theory.

Instead, I reached for his hand.

He blinked, then let me hold it.

"I don't want you to think I'm pulling away," I whispered. "I just... there's something I need to figure out before I drag you into it."

Aaron's grip tightened. "Isa, whatever it is—you won't face it alone."

I asked him to stop calling me Lilith.

I swallowed hard. "I know."

And I wanted to believe that. I did. But deep down, I also knew something else.

Later That Night

I waited until Aaron had retreated

Then I unwrapped the book again.

Page by page, I searched for clues I might've missed. Symbols. Annotations. A thread to pull.

Halfway through, I found it.

A single page had been folded inward. Tucked inside was a sliver of faded envelope paper with a note.

And beside the note, written in the margin, was a single phrase circled in that same blood-red ink:

"Mercy is wasted on gods."

The line sent a shiver down my spine.

It wasn't random.

Leo or whoever it was hadn't just left me a trail. He was testing me. Pushing me. And the game wasn't about information—it was about timing.

How long could I hold out before I told someone?

Before I broke?

I slid the book back into the hiding space beneath the floorboard, careful not to wake Aaron.

When I turned to look at him, still asleep under the soft glow of the kitchen lamp, something twisted in my chest.

He was everything the world wasn't.

Warm.

But Leo, if he was NSSA—then no one I cared about was safe. Not even Aaron.

Especially not Aaron.

The next morning, I found Aaron at the stove.

He glanced over his shoulder when he heard me. "Didn't want to wake you."

"That's becoming a habit," I murmured.

"Some habits are worth keeping." He smiled.

I sat at the table, watching him. There were tiny things about him I hadn't noticed before—like how he always tapped the spoon twice against the rim after stirring coffee, or how he never checked his phone before I did. It all felt... intentional.

But I didn't question it.

Because Aaron had been there when I needed grounding. When the house went quiet. When I forgot how to sleep. When I couldn't speak.

And now?

Now I couldn't tell him I was unraveling again.

He set the plate in front of me. "Eat. You're running on fumes."

I picked up the fork and pushed the food around my plate. " Aaron, Evelyn was hurt because of me, because I was close to her, they might try to harm you, but don't die. Not yet."

Aaron's brow furrowed faintly.

"TMI" he smiled.

"Huh? " I know it might be TMI (Too Much Information) for him but I wanted to trust him maybe these lines were not for him but me, they were to assure my trust more than for his safety.

He just sat across from me, elbows on the table, eyes dark and steady. "You don't have to carry this alone."

I offered a brittle smile. "I'm not alone."

And for a few seconds, I believed it.

Then my phone buzzed.

No caller ID.

One image.

No message this time.

Just a picture of the same book—Names of God—but opened to a different page.

I frowned and rolled my eyes

Aaron noticed.

"Who is it?" he asked.

Looking up from the screen of his mobile phone.

"No one," I lied. "Spam."

But I saved the image before deleting it from my screen.

Because it wasn't spam.

It was a warning.

Or a reminder.

Or both.

That Evening – Vincent's Apartment

I met Vincent just after dusk. His windows were open, blinds drawn tight, the scent of bitter espresso hanging in the air like smoke.

He didn't waste time.

"Where did you find the book?"

"Used bookstore. Hidden."

He nodded slowly. "That handwriting—on the back of the photo. I've seen it before."

I froze. "Where?"

Vincent pulled out an old file. Yellowed edges. Dust still clinging to the clasp. He opened it like a priest reading last rites.

Inside was a report—never filed. Water-damaged, partly burned. It was from the fire.

And next to the report, clipped in place, was a letter. Dated two days before the explosion.

Signed: Leo M.

My stomach turned.

"He was there?" I whispered. "Before the shooting?"

Vincent nodded. "And according to this... he wasn't just there."

He looked up at me, eyes sharp.

"He started it."

I took a step. "No... he wouldn't—he was Astrid's friend."

"Friends turn," Vincent said grimly. "Especially when they think they've been forgotten."

I sank into the chair, trembling.

Aaron had told me once—months ago—that the worst kind of enemy was the one who thought they were doing the right thing.

What if Leo believed this was righteous?

What if NSSA wasn't just seeking revenge—but validation?

Later – Home Again

Aaron wasn't on the couch when I returned.

The apartment was quiet again—but this time, it wasn't comforting.

A breeze moved through the cracked window.

I turned.

He was on the balcony, arms crossed, back to me.

When I stepped out, he didn't turn.

"Something's bothering you," he said, not a question.

I didn't answer.

Because it wasn't just something.

It was everything.

I stood beside him, watching the city blur below.

He spoke first. "I know you don't tell me everything. You don't have to. But I need you to know something."

I turned to him, uncertain.

Aaron looked over, eyes steady, voice quiet.

"I would never hurt you, Isa. Never."

The breath caught in my throat.

"I know," I whispered.

And I meant it.

Because whatever secrets I was chasing—whatever ghost from my past had clawed its way back—I knew Aaron wasn't the monster.

He was the reason I hadn't become one.

I stared at the Chrysanthemum vase. It's almost permanent now.

CHAPTER EIGHT

AT THE ALLEY

I sat behind a box rack in an alley with almost three... no four hollow meat sacks, even though we were the ones who did this. How? Well here's a flashback.

Two Hours Earlier

The plan was simple.

To get records so we can reach NSSA.

Get in. Grab the ledger. Don't leave a trace. No names, no sound, no blood.

That last part didn't stick.

Vincent had eyes on the west exit, earpiece crackling with interference as he murmured, "Two guards, same pattern. Thirty-second gap."

Aaron was already inside. A shadow against the servers, fingers moving too fast, too precise. That's how I knew it wasn't his first time. I didn't ask where he learned that.

Me?

I played bait.

Red dress, black heels. I mean I can't go to a club looking harmless if I wore my coat and my usual fit, I'd look like I am in the mafia, well I was technically.

I walked into the casino.

The guard on the left— was Matteo, I think. I leaned against the bar, ordered something with a weird name, and counted to forty-two.

When I stood up, Matteo stood too. Right on cue.

I had to take the ledger while Matteo guided me. He was known to Vincent.

Then everything went to hell.

Back to the Alley

"Plan was simple," I muttered, dragging my nail along the cement.

Aaron crouched beside one of the bodies, checking for a pulse we both knew wasn't there.

"They weren't supposed to be armed," I said.

"They weren't supposed to be dead," he shot back.

Vincent lit a cigarette with shaking fingers, not from guilt—but anticipation. "One of them said something before he went out. 'He knows.' That was it."

"Who?" I asked.

Vincent met my eyes. "You tell me."

I looked back at the blood. At the splatter on the concrete. At the way none of them even fought back properly—like they knew this was coming. Like they wanted it.

And then I remembered what was missing.

The ledger.

It wasn't there.

Because someone beat us to it.

Because someone knew we were coming.

Because this whole thing... wasn't a heist.

It was bait.

And we swallowed it.

"NSSA, he tried to distract us, he might be stirring up a ruckus by now"

I sighed.

"Bored?" Aaron asked me.

"How long do we wait until they clear up the mess?"

"Pick up that," he said pointing at the newspaper pile, "Kill your time"

"Yeah, else she'll kill us" I smirked as Aaron said that.

"TMI"

I said as I let out a chuckle. Then I looked at the newspaper's name. 'Theodore'

"IMT"

Now, I know who to be wary of. Everyone.

Two nights earlier.

Vincent and I had followed the trail Evelyn left us. Not breadcrumbs—blood. Each name she dropped had been part of the Springfield Echelon, but every lead led to another corpse. Only this time, they weren't dead when we arrived. Not yet.

We cornered them in a forgotten tenement, the kind that smelled like rot and secrets. Vincent went to the second floor. I stayed below, pistol tucked behind my back.

They begged. Of course they did.

I remember the youngest one shaking so hard his teeth clicked. I asked him who sent the package—who delivered the severed hands.

Yes, that photo was taken from France and was delivered to someone's house. The cufflink was deliberate, NSSA did not click the picture. We have our ways to find it out.

He said he didn't know.

I shot him anyway.

Vincent didn't flinch. He never does.

The others broke faster after that. Told us what they knew. It wasn't much, but enough to stitch the pieces together:

NSSA had been using aliases—more than one. Each message from NSSA was routed through dead IPs, burned proxies, or clean servers last accessed from state hospitals, morgues, or—worst of all—places I knew.

Places we'd been.

He was always a step ahead because he had already walked the path.

Present day.

Vincent leaned against the wall of the alley now, wiping his blade on the sleeve of a man whose name we never got. I crouched, breathing through it.

My palms were sticky. My ears rang.

I had done this before.

But it was different when I wasn't sure if we were still the good guys.

"Isa," Vincent said, quieter than usual, "you okay?"

I looked at him, then at the bodies.

"We're not done."

He nodded. "Figured."

We burned the alley.

Vincent soaked the walls in accelerant while I gathered everything we had touched—shell casings, ropes, stray hairs, footprints in blood. The lighter felt almost theatrical, but we had no time for it. He lit it, dropped it, and we stood in the shadows as the flames devoured what we left behind.

The stench of burning flesh clawed into my nostrils. I didn't flinch. Neither did he.

I didn't ask if it was too much. We couldn't risk fingerprints. Or memory.

Later, as we drove back, I stared at the streetlights flickering past.

"We ever think maybe Evelyn's not dead?" I asked, voice low.

Vincent didn't look at me. "You saw the photo."

"I've seen worse fakes."

He glanced over. "You want her to be alive?"

I didn't answer.

He took that as a yes.

Aaron was asleep again when I returned. His face was peaceful. Unbothered. I envied that.

I closed the door softly and headed to the bathroom. Washed my hands. Watched the red swirl down the drain and vanish like none of it had happened.

Except it had.

I stared at myself in the mirror.

The blood wasn't just on my skin.

It was in me now.

Every life I'd taken. Every order I'd followed. Every truth I'd rewritten to keep breathing.

NSSA wasn't playing a game anymore.

He was forcing me to remember the one I had already played.

And lost.

The next morning, I got another message.

NSSA-You're doing well. Just like old times.

My stomach turned.

I picked up the book again—Names of God. Flipped to a page I hadn't noticed before.

There it was. Scribbled in pencil.

"She bled for the truth. And then she drowned in it."

The handwriting matched. From the photo. From the old letters I never threw away.

There was no doubt now.

He wasn't just tracking me.

He was narrating me.

And if he was, that meant he knew what came next.

And so did I.

More blood.

But this time, maybe not just theirs.

Maybe mine too.

Vincent was gone when I woke up.

Just a note, folded three times and stabbed into the wood of the kitchen table with one of my own knives.

"Don't follow. Don't trust the girl in the photo."

The photo?

I dug through the evidence box, fingers trembling. There were dozens of them—crime scenes, autopsy shots, old surveillance reels—but only one that fit. The hospital room. The mirror.

There was someone reflected in it. Someone I hadn't noticed before.

Blonde hair. Gloved hands. A scar under her eye.

I scanned it into my system, traced the outline, enhanced it ten different ways before the program locked in a face.

Eloise Thorne.

Alive.

I stared at the morgue log again. Same signature. But now I know what to look for.

It wasn't a name—it was a tag. A handler's signature. Like a puppeteer's initials burned into his marionette.

I hadn't just been rewritten.

I had been directed.

Vincent was gone when I woke up.

Just a note, folded three times and stabbed into the wood of the kitchen table with one of my own knives.

"Don't follow. Don't trust the girl in the photo."

The photo?

I dug through the evidence box, fingers trembling. There were dozens of them—crime scenes, autopsy shots, old surveillance reels—but only one that fit. The hospital room. The mirror.

There was someone reflected in it. Someone I hadn't noticed before.

Blonde hair. Gloved hands. A scar under her eye.

I scanned it into my system, traced the outline, enhanced it ten different ways before the program locked in a face.

Eloise Thorne.

Alive.

I stared at the morgue log again. Same signature. But now I know what to look for.

It wasn't a name—it was a tag. A handler's signature. Like a puppeteer's initials burned into his marionette.

I hadn't just been rewritten.

I had been directed.

I booked a ticket to Marseille under a dead alias and left Aaron sleeping.

I didn't even write a note.

I couldn't look him in the eye—not until I knew for sure he hadn't known.

Because if he had...

If he had stood beside me while I murdered and burned and bled my way through half of Springfield, and known?

I couldn't survive that betrayal.

Not again.

France.

It smelled like cigarettes and rot and too many winters behind stone walls.

I found her.

Eloise.

Alive, and aging. Or maybe just waiting.

She didn't look surprised to see me.

"I wondered when you'd come," she said, voice brittle as wire.

"You're supposed to be dead," I said, gun hidden in my coat.

She didn't flinch. "Aren't we all?"

I slammed the photo on the table. "Why was Theodore in the morgue that night? Why did he sign your death?"

Here's the revised version with the reveal leaning toward Leo being the man in the photo—all while keeping it eerie, tension-packed, and faithful to your story's tone:

"Sign your death?"

She tapped the edge of her glass. "He was never signing mine, darling. He was signing yours."

"What?"

Her eyes were black lakes. "That bed. That girl in the mirror. That wasn't me."

My pulse roared.

"You're saying—"

"I'm saying," she interrupted, "that you were meant to stay under. But Astrid brought you out too soon."

Astrid.

My brother.

The one who died.

Eloise slid something across the table.

A photo. Crumpled. Almost too old to read.

It was of *him*.

Unrecognisable—burned at the edges. His mouth mid-speech, arms stiff at his sides.

He was standing next to someone whose face had been blurred—intentionally.

PROJECT SALIENT – CLEARANCE RED.

My fingers curled. My throat dried.

We were the only ones—me and my brother—who'd ever seen each other as children and adults.

And even though the face was smeared... I knew.

It was Leo, the one my brother was talking to.

Something in the tilt of his shoulder.

The gloved hand.

The way he stood—like everything around him was disposable.

Back at the hotel, I smashed the mirror.

Glass cracked like nerves.

Behind the frame—a USB drive. Tucked into a clean cutout.

As if someone expected I'd find it.

Someone had been in here before me.

I plugged it into my laptop, jaw locked. My brain wasn't working on logic anymore. This wasn't about malware.

This was about answers.

There were files.

Footage.

Me.

Strapped to a hospital bed.

Thrashing. Screaming. Sedated.

A nurse whispered, "Subject 7 is destabilizing."

Doctors arguing off-screen.

A voice I almost remembered. Calm. Measured. "No more memories. Let her forget."

Then came the final clip.

A nameplate on a scorched office door.

EO

And below it—stamped into a burned intake form:

ISADORA LEMAIRE – SUBJECT 7

My ears rang. My breath stopped. The drive ejected itself automatically.

But one last folder opened on its own.

A single image.

A man.

Smiling. Menacingly.

Wearing the same gloves The gloves I knew.

The smile I'd seen in a hundred careless moments.

Leo.

Theo?

CHAPTER NINE

PROJECT SALIENT

NSSA- Subject Seven's spine of glass,
    Cracked by love and tied with brass.
    Eyes that close remember sin,
    Open wide — let blood begin.
ME- Nice. You know.
NSSA- I always have.

I headed to the room where I had kept Eloise, she's useful.

I spiked her drink and brought her here, I mean what was I supposed to do, she wasn't agreeing to come with me.

About a day ago.

"Come with me, to Paris," I huffed.

"I already left that work"

"Start it again, then?" I made a face.

I spiked her coffee and brought her here, explaining it is too much.

Back to present

"Hi!" I exclaimed

"Want something?" I asked, crossing my arms and leaning against the doorframe. "Food? Wine? Something not drugged this time, promise."

She didn't answer.

I stepped forward slowly. "I need your help."

"Your way of asking is... creative," she muttered.

I smirked, but my heart wasn't in it. "Yeah, well, creativity's all I have left."

Eloise took a slow sip of the wine.

"You're still chasing ghosts, you know."

"I'm chasing truth," I shot back.

She tilted her head. "You always thought Salient was about your memories. The things they took. But that's just what they let you believe."

I froze. "What are you talking about?"

Eloise leaned forward. Her voice dropped.

"Project Salient wasn't about what they took from you. It was about what they put in you."

I stared.

She continued. "You think they just erased your trauma? No, darling. They engineered who you became."

I shook my head, slowly at first. "No. They sedated us. They controlled—"

"No. They tested you. Broke you down. Watched how you rebuilt yourself. Over and over." Her tone sharpened. "Salient was designed to find candidates—people who didn't flinch when morality cracked. Not memory wipes. Moral architecture. Psychological recoding."

I felt my stomach churn.

"They built us to be..."

"Performers," Eloise said, cruelly calm. "Sympathetic infiltrators. You weren't supposed to survive that final phase. You did. You weren't supposed to remember. But look at you now."

"Why me?" I whispered.

She smiled, bitter and beautiful.

"Because you were salient, Isa. Exceptionally noticeable. Exceptionally lethal."

So the handler, he was Leo?

I knew it. Who NSSA was. But no, I couldn't reveal it yet.

I looked at Eloise.

Time to game up.

I need to find out about Project Salient first.

What it was, why was it and how, I ended up as a subject in it.

I sank in the hot water bath, after taking a handful of sleeping pills as always, maybe it's an overdose, but I did it so much that I no longer cared.

Sometimes I envy the fan,
Why can it hang so freely?

Today I felt it once more.
Just how alone I was in this.
No one to trust.
No one to rely.
Not now, just never.
I closed my eyes.

Tried to count the cracks in my memory like the ones in the ceiling.
Tried to breathe like the pills hadn't already softened the edges of my lungs.
Tried to forget the mirror. The one I shattered last week. The one I caught myself talking to.

Sometimes I wonder if I'm really alone...
Or if I'm the ghost that haunts me.

The water cooled slowly.
Time stretched.

And then, just before sleep dragged me under,
I saw it.

Not with my eyes.
With the part of me they never broke.

A flash.
A memory, sharp and uninvited.

Someone holding a syringe.
A name whispered behind mirrored glass.
Not mine.

"Subject Seven has stabilized."
"Keep the memories layered."
"We need to see what she chooses on her own."

My heart skipped.
Then another flash—
     A shadow by the hospital bed.
Gloved hands.
That same faint cologne I caught on a shirt once, but couldn't place.
     Couldn't place... or refused to?
     The fan kept spinning.
My brain didn't.
     I lurched up, water splashing over the sides.
Shivering now, because the warmth had turned cold—and I'd just
remembered why I never stayed in too long.
     Too much silence, and things came back.
     I staggered to the mirror despite the fractured glass.
I looked like someone else in the shards.
A woman carved in layers.
Built. Bent. Rewritten.
     And still bleeding at the seams.
     If Project Salient was about moral reconstruction—
What else had they reconstructed in me?
     My hands shook.
     I needed to find the others.
The other Subjects.
     If they were still alive, they'd remember.
And if they didn't—
     Then I wasn't meant to remember either.
     I walked barefoot across the tiles, each step a quiet declaration.
Pulled on the coat that still smelled like fear and steel.
And as I reached for the door—
     My phone buzzed.
     UNKNOWN NUMBER:
She's awake.
     Just two words. No name.
     But I knew who they meant.
And worse—
     I knew who sent it.

I should've deleted it.

I didn't.

Aaron moved back to the states five days ago.

Instead, I slipped the phone into my pocket, grabbed the knife I kept taped under the sink, and walked into the night like the monster they made me.

I reached there, a girl.

Too young at that.

Wait.

Don't tell me.

She handed me a scarf with a note, which I have kept with me till date, as a reminder.

Christmas is in two days.

Need to clear this mess up before... No. On Christmas.

A gift to my brother.

A tribute to everyone I ever loved.

This is the last game. But not before Christmas Eve's celebration.

The apartment was glowing, soft and warm, the kind of warmth that didn't quite reach the bones but fooled the skin just enough to make you stay a little longer. The smell of cinnamon and cloves curled around everything—the drapes, the pages of books left half-read on the coffee table, the rim of the glasses that lined the kitchen counter.

Candles lined at the fireplace mantle, their light swaying gently in the hush of the room. Shadows danced over a worn photo frame I had moved that morning—carefully, deliberately. It held a picture of my brother and me, back when we were just kids playing grown-up with cameras and too much trust in the world. He had his arm around me, wide-eyed and grinning, like the future was nothing more than a firework waiting to go off but it does erode at some point doesn't it?. "I love this time of year, snow makes the city feel like a secret. That it buried everything ugly and let you pretend, even for a day, that nothing had ever gone wrong."

A note from him at the back of the frame.

The scarf she'd handed me— from Eloise, was draped loosely around my wrist. Its threads were fraying now, but the note inside, folded into fourths and tucked into my pocket, hadn't left me since she gave it. A reminder. A promise. Or maybe a warning.

Christmas was in two days.
I'd clear the mess then—not before.
That day would belong to him.
To everyone I failed.
One final move. One last truth.
And then, silence.

But tonight?
Tonight I was Isadora who still knew how to smile. The gracious host. The woman who could light a dozen candles and hide a storm behind every single flame.

I invited Vincent. I invited Aaron.

"Just something small," I'd said, my voice calm and warm, the way I imagined someone would say if they had nothing to hide. "A quiet little evening. To feel less alone before the year ends."

They said yes without hesitation.

Vincent brought two bottles of fruit juice, I asked him to, he carried that stupid, familiar grin that meant he was pretending things were fine. He wore a dark turtleneck and forgot to brush his hair. He always did that when he was nervous. Or guilty. Or both.

Aaron arrived twenty minutes late, apologizing with a crooked smile and a ridiculous story about a cab driver who couldn't read GPS, how they'd gone in circles while he gave up and enjoyed the view.

We laughed. We toasted. I wore blood red.

For a few hours, it almost felt real.
Like the world outside the windows didn't exist.
Like we were just three weary souls making room for joy in a year that had stolen too much.

We sank into the couch, plates balanced on knees, shoulders pressed together in that easy way we used to sit after long nights of chasing names and breaking codes. We talked about the things people talk about when they're trying not to touch the real things: holiday songs, favorite memories, old scars dressed up as stories.

Aaron said Last Christmas was the only right answer. Vincent argued for Carol of the bells , I said nothing. I just poured more of the fruit juice, nodded when they teased, laughed when they expected me to.

I watched them with something like affection. Or grief. Or the stillness before a storm.

No one at that table knew what tomorrow held.
I wanted to be with my only family for the last two years.

To everyone I ever cared for.
To memory.
To the part of me still human.

CHAPTER TEN

TMI?

The room was dim.

Concrete walls, one flickering bulb overhead. A single chair in the center. Another one, bolted to the floor. Restraints like they were always meant to be there. A table with tools—not sharp enough to kill, just enough to remind.

I moved slowly.I'd done this before.
Because I had.

The air buzzed with the silence of old machines. No one would hear screams here. Not anymore.

One of them was already awake—his wrists straining against the bonds in slow, rhythmic pulses. Breathing labored. Head bowed.

The other?

Still out cold. For now.

I leaned forward, brushing a strand of hair from the sleeping one's face. Familiar. Too familiar. But I couldn't let myself feel that. Not yet.

I pressed the tip of a finger to his temple, tracing the faint bruise blooming there. A sigh escaped me, too soft to be heard.

"Remember me, even though I have to go, remember me"....
"No," I whispered, almost gently.
"Remember me, even though I have to make you go, remember me"-
"didn't you sing the same Astrid when you shot me?"

The other man stirred. Flinched. Eyes blinking into focus like someone pulling themselves up from the bottom of a very deep, very dark sea.

No recognition yet. Just panic. Then pain. Then—questions.

I stepped back into the shadowed part of the room, near the wall where a camera used to be. It had long since stopped recording.

He coughed, finally lifting his face.

Blood dried at the corner of his mouth. But his smile... crooked. Resistant.

"Still playing games?" he rasped.

I tilted my head. "No. This isn't a game anymore."

His expression faltered. A pause in his breath.

And then I saw it.

The crack.

He remembered.

But I didn't let it register. Not yet. I turned to the second captive instead—newly conscious, blinking like someone caught in a dream.

He looked at me.

And I let him.

Let the silence settle.

Let them both wonder how long I'd known.

How long I'd planned this.

Let the ghost of my brother's voice echo through the room like frost creeping under skin.

Because tonight, there was no turning back.

Only answers.

And agony.

The silence between us had teeth.

Astrid's breathing had gone shallow, and the other man—still blinking, dazed—tried to move his arms.

But the cuffs were tight. Too tight.

This place had been soundproofed long before I found it. I'd just... personalized it.

Made it mine.

I walked to the table against the wall. Let my fingers hover over the collection there—small, neat, deliberate.

Then I picked up the pliers.

Not the rusted kind. These were clean. Precise.

Because this wasn't about infection.

His eyes followed the movement. His voice cracked when he spoke.

"You know what this is?" I said pointing at the pliers.

"You don't have to do this."

I smiled softly. "No. I really don't."

I crouched beside him. Pressed the cold metal to his index finger.

"But you should've told me before I had to say it. Before I remembered everything from my past two memory losses."

His body tensed. Still defiant. Still pretending to be brave.

I pulled out his index finger's nail.

"It's just one," I whispered, like I was promising a gift. "For Vincent."

And then I pulled.

The scream tore through the room like it was ripping cloth—and something in the other man woke all at once.

Eyes wide. Breathing hitched.

He knew. Or was beginning to.

I dropped the nail on the floor between them with a soft clink.

"One down," I said, standing.

"No more games. Just names. Truth. And pain."

"Aww Astrid don't cry"

"Wondering how I know?"

"I knew everything from the day I woke up from the five week sleep, I was just wishing you'd say the truth before I had to pull out your nails."

Just then someone hissed.

"Aaron!" I squealed.

"IMT, this time"

"Isadora Missed Theodore" I said.

"What? I am not dumb Aaron nor slow. TMI?" I continued, "Huh?"

"Now tell me how, should I address you?".. "Your options are Neuro-Sensory Stimulation Algorithm or was it Aaron (NSSA),

Theodore, or my beloved Aaron"

Aaron—Theodore—closed his eyes for a breath. Just one. Like maybe the darkness behind his lids would offer a way out. It didn't. When he opened them, I was still there, crouched between them, pliers in one hand, blood on my glove, resolve in my eyes.

I turned the pliers in my hand slowly, watching the way his gaze flicked between the tool and my face. "This is consequence."

Astrid let out a low groan from behind, coughing against the metallic taste of memory and blood. His head lolled forward. "She's serious, man..."

"Do you know what he did?" I asked Astrid, not looking at him. "What he really did?"

"I—I don't know," Astrid stammered.

"But you did," I said softly, cutting through his denial like a scalpel. "You knew enough to shut your mouth and turn your back. That's all it takes to be complicit."

I looked back at Aaron.

"You took my brother," I whispered, the words a curse wrapped in silk. "And then you had the gall to stand beside me. To play protector. Pretend to mourn him with me."

He didn't answer. But his silence wasn't strength—it was guilt. Heavy. Cold. A ghost settling onto his shoulders.

I moved again. This time to his middle finger.

"I cared for you... you both, maybe not well defined... but we were family," I said, more to myself now. "In whatever warped way I was capable of. That's the real tragedy, isn't it?"

Click.

The pliers locked around the nail.

"No—wait," Aaron croaked.

I didn't pull. Not yet.

"Then speak," I said, freezing the moment. "Give me one thing. One truth. One reason why I shouldn't peel every lie from your body the way you peeled pieces off mine."

He looked up at me, his face bloodied, his breath shaking.

And finally, Aaron whispered, "Because I didn't kill Vincent."

I stared.

Astrid blinked hard, lifting his head.

"I know".

I stood still. Not blinking. Not breathing.

Astrid said quietly, "He's lying."

"No," I said. "He's not."

"But you're still NSSA," I said. "You still misguided me.Killed the ones close to me, manipulated me into-"

Aaron nodded, barely.

"And you still let me believe I was crazy."

I released the pliers.

But I wasn't done.

"You won't die tonight," I told him. "That would be too easy."

I looked between them. Astrid's breathing shallow. Aaron's eyes wide and covered with a fear he'd never admit to.

"You're both going to live long enough to see what I become next."

Then I smiled.

Because I already knew what I was going to do.

And I had no intention of stopping.

Now, you must ask how they're here?

Huh? Are you all that dumb to not see it ... well let me take you back in time, that time when I slipped into a five week long mild coma, it was not just a coma, it was quite like a recovery... memory recovery, I had known ever since, who they were. What they sought for. But not Aaron being NSSA. That was discovered through his TMI.

The Too Much Information he gave me, but back then this acronym didn't carry the same meaning, ...it meant "Theodore Missed Isadora"

I didn't know it back then, but back at the alley, when my eyes caught the glimpse of the newspaper named 'Theodore'.

The dots connected and here we are.

That was when I knew who I was looking for.

And the next one. Oh don't.

The pin.

About who killed my brother, you will know in time.

Now, you must be wondering—how are they here?

Huh? Are you all really that blind?

Fine. Let me take you back in time. To when I slipped into a five-week-long mild coma.

Only... it wasn't just a coma. It was more like a reset. A recovery. A memory recovery.

I had known ever since.

Who they were.

What they wanted.

But not Aaron.

Not that he was NSSA.

That came later. Through his TMI.

That's when I knew.

Who I was really looking for.

And the next one—

Oh, don't.

I put Astrid and Aaron in different rooms.

I went to my favourite room, and there he sat. Aaron.

He smiled again.

That same smile — infuriating, languid.

The pliers in my hand weren't heavy from blood. They were heavy from being ignored. From being insufficient.

"You're bleeding," I told him, voice flat.

"I am," Aaron murmured, eyes on the dark red puddle pooling near his boot. "So dramatic. You always had a flair for theatre, Isa."

Crack.

The metal jaws of the pliers twisted around his pinky and snapped the bone sideways. His scream tore the silence—

—and broke into laughter halfway through.

God, he was still laughing.

"You think pain brings the truth?" he panted once it passed. "You think I was the one pretending?"

I grabbed his jaw and forced him to meet my eyes.

"You lied to me for three years. Lied to everyone. For what?"

He grinned wider, blood flecked across his teeth.

"I never lied, Isadora. I just never told you everything."

I pulled the chair closer, crouching at eye level, letting him see what was left in my eyes.

"Then tell me now."

He didn't blink.

"No."

I smiled. Slowly.

Then brought the gun to my own temple.

"Speak," I said.

Silence.

His eyes tracked the movement — not with fear, but with something worse. Fascination. Like he was watching a star implode.

"You wouldn't," he said finally.

I slammed the hammer back., The sound echoed like thunder.

"Speak. Or I redecorate this room with the last thing you'll ever see."

Aaron tilted his head — blood dripping from his temple, his smile like a cracked mask.

"You're insane," he murmured.

I leaned in.

"I learned from the best."

I took the my Springfield Echelon to my temple, and played the most dramitically convincing scene."I am tired of it Aaron, so I will end it here in front of you, the weapon you've protected to use in war. On the count of three"

For the first time, he wavered.

I could feel it. The silence shifted. Something coiled tight inside him — not fear for me, but a fear of silence. Of not being heard. Of not being understood before I slipped away with the bullet.

So I held his gaze.

"Three seconds," I said. "Three."

He watched me.

"Two."

A twitch. His jaw locked.

"One."

"I'm NSSA," he snapped. Voice low. Like a secret he hated letting go.

"I've always been."

Click.

I lowered the gun.

What? You thought I'll kill myself?

I knew just how to tick him off. He didn't want me to die, not in front in him. I was the reason he kept living after all.

My heart didn't slow.

"You're lying."

"I'm not," he said. "You think someone could fake that name? Mimic every move? Every message? I've bled for that code. I've buried bodies for it. I designed half of the puzzles you solved just to reach me."

I stared at him.

"You were a child when we met—" he continued, breath shallow but steady. "You were wearing a navy-blue coat."

I rolled my eyes.

"Oh, how poetic. Going down memory lane now?"

He didn't flinch. "Thirteen. Gold lion buttons. And that woman — , I remember that much. She held your hand like she thought letting go would set the world on fire."

I tilted my head. "Is this meant to impress me?"

"No," he said, smiling through the blood on his teeth. "It's meant to remind you. That I've known longer than you think. I saw you before the legend. Before the bodies. Before the chrysanthemums."

I leaned in, pliers still warm in my grip.

"And you thought that gave you ownership? Congratulations, Aaron. You were a stalker with a badge."

"I was your worshipper."

I scoffed. "You sound like a cultist."

He didn't deny it. "Maybe I was. You were more than rumor, more than shadow."

I smiled. Cold. Clean. Mean

"Though, I was quite surprised when I first met you."

"I break bones," I whispered, pressing the pliers against his jawline. "Not hearts."

His breath hitched — only slightly.

"Funny," I added. "You remember my coat, but not the fact that I've been three steps ahead of you this entire time."

"You think this is about a game?" he hissed.

I met his eyes, flat.

"No. I think this is about a boy who saw a girl in a navy coat at an orphanage and decided that meant she culd be turned into his lethal war weapon and belonged to him."

Crack.

The pliers closed again — this time on his cheek, flesh tearing like paper.

He winced. But only for a second.

Then he laughed again, choking on it.

"You still don't get it," he said, voice raw. "You're the storm they tried to dress in silk. I just wanted to see you unleashed."

I stepped back, face blank.

"Careful what you wish for."

He was still laughing when I pressed the tip of the pliers under his chin.

"Speak again," I said coldly, "and I'll rip the smile off your face this time."

Aaron's laughter dimmed — but not gone. Not entirely. He swallowed hard, blood dripping down his cheek like sweat, and met my eyes with something almost reverent.

"You want to know why I joined the mafia?" he rasped.

"Because therapy was too expensive?" I shot back.

But he kept going — of course he did.

"I joined the mafia years later. Circumstance. Survival. But the first time I heard of 'Chrysanthemums,' my breath caught. A ghost of a name. A killer who left flowers instead of footprints. I followed the pattern. Obsessed over it. I thought, finally—someone who sees the world the way I do."

"And then?" I asked, voice low.

"And then," he whispered, "I saw you."

"You weren't a ghost anymore. You weren't myth. You were real. But you weren't...her. Not entirely. Not then. You were someone's sister. Someone's pawn. You were so used to get permitted. And I hated that. Hated that you, that dagger in the dark, didn't know you were the one holding the blade."

"So you decided to help," I said, voice soaked in venom.

"No"

I crossed my arms, unimpressed. "So you fell in love with a fantasy story?"-"You harmed *the wrong brother Aaron.*"

"No," he said, voice low now. "I fell in *obsession.* I thought she was a myth, a message. Until one day, I found a file."

My hand twitched.

"A name redacted. An image blurred. But the shape, the stance... it was you. I didn't know it then. But I'd seen that girl before."

He nodded. "I chased that photo through syndicates, through brokers, through blood. And I kept finding her. The woman with a garden of corpses. I thought I was hunting a phantom. I didn't realize..."

His voice dropped even further.

"...that I was chasing the same girl I'd seen standing above us orphans like a ghost."

I tilted my head.

"So imagine your surprise when your perfect killer turned out to be little Isadora," I said, sarcastic.

He rolled his eyes.

"When I realized it was you. When I understood that the girl with the velvet gloves and glass eyes was the one who made monsters flinch."

His voice held no sarcasm now.

"I didn't want to stop you. I wanted to understand you."

"By becoming NSSA?" I rose my brows.

"By becoming the only one worthy of reaching you." he, calmer this time.

Starting from the very beginning he narrated a tale so known yet so far so close but hazy.

His eyes never left mine, and for a moment, I saw it—pride. Not regret. Not guilt. Pride.

"I watched you, Isadora," he said, softly. "You had all the makings of her. The stillness. The calculation. That grief-drenched fury you kept folding into silence. But you were too busy chasing your brothers' shadows. Too busy waiting for someone else to give you permission."

My jaw clenched.

"And I thought, *what a waste*. What a waste of something so precise. So inevitable.You didn't need their say in it. You just didn't know it yet."

My fingers curled into fists, but I didn't speak. Not yet.

"So I gave you a story," he went on, his voice almost reverent. "A little nightmare. A little blood. Something to crack the surface."

"In the past I tried to remove your brothers from your life at once, but you resisted it even though you know they betrayed you."

"You gave me a corpse," I said.

He smiled faintly. "No. I gave you a mirror."

I took a step closer, shadows wrapping around me like the ghosts he thought he'd buried.

"First Vincent and now,"-"You killed that man," I hissed.

"You killed the only people who were never bad to me," I said, voice cold, yet shaking. "The only ones who treated me like family without wanting something in return."

His silence was louder than any confession. But I wasn't done.

"You think you awakened me," I hissed, stepping closer. "But all you did was hollow me out further. Tear apart the last place I had warmth."

A flicker of confusion crossed his face.

"I'm not talking about Vincent. Or anyone else ," I clarified, jaw clenched. "You remember that company representative? "

His eyes shifted. Recognition. Regret.

The time when I was Subject Seven-

The corridor lights buzzed above us—too white, too sterile. Like everything in this place, it made the air feel colder than it should've been. My boots echoed softly against the concrete floor, yet his footsteps remained silent. He walked beside me with a kind of practiced stillness, like someone who'd learned to make himself invisible in full view.

We didn't speak until the door closed behind us.

Then he turned. The white badge clipped to his coat caught the light—Project Salient: Tier IV Access.

I glanced at it, then at him.

He worked there.

I just don't remember the exact position. Only that it mattered. He had clearance higher than most, and he moved like someone used to doors unlocking before he reached them. Maybe he was part of the core, or maybe just close enough to it that no one questioned why he took extra brad with him each day.

To them, he was just fulfilling his duty—bringing me meals, reporting my stability, adjusting the variables.

To me... he was the only one who didn't look at me like I was a test. From then on I named him *Sunshine.*

He never flinched when I wouldn't speak. Never rushed when I did. He'd leave an extra slice of bread on the tray when he thought no one was watching. Sometimes he'd sit for a moment longer than necessary, like he wanted to say something but wasn't sure if I'd understand it.

Or if he'd survive it.

"I used to be in the dark too," he said once. Quiet. Like a prayer. "But you—you're not meant to stay there."

And maybe I should've known then.

Maybe I should've guessed.

The first time he slipped me a folded page under my tray.

I didn't ask what it meant. He didn't explain.

We didn't need to. I knew I couldn't escape it.

But kindness has a scent, and like all things sweet, it rots if left exposed too long.

They found out.

Not all of it. Just enough. That he lingered longer than protocol. That the cameras sometimes cut off near my chamber for minutes at a time. That I was eating better than I should've been.

They reassigned him.

No. Not reassigned—deposed.

From handler to subject.

Subject Eight.

When they dragged him out of the administrative wing and into the lower floor, I heard the boots from my cot. Heard him fight. Heard someone scream for backup. Heard the silence after.

I didn't see him for three weeks.

And when I finally did, he wasn't wearing the silver pin on his lapel anymore. He was in white now. Like me. Like the others. Like property.

But he didn't look at me with resentment.

He looked at me like he always had.

Like I was the only real thing in that place.

"Why?" I whispered when I passed him in the observation hallway, monitored but just far enough for a breath of conversation.

His answer came quickly.

"Because you mattered before they told you, you didn't."

And it stayed with me.

Even after they took his name from the system.

Even after he vanished from the daily rosters.

Even after I found his file blacked out in the archive drawer labeled Failed Attempts.

He didn't fail me.

I failed him.

Because I survived and he didn't.

Because he died because he wanted to save me. He wanted to remind me after he remembered.

Because I remembered, too late, that he was the first one who ever tried to set me free without asking for anything in return.

And the last one to treat me human.

Andthe death of my brother was another case.

"You thought they weakened me, no they were the sole reason I kept living..." I said calmer now.

I got up and left the room, I needed to deal with *my brother.*

You must be wondering how I was talking to Astrid, well he never died. The one who died was Vincent and the one who was with me in France all along was not Vincent, he was Astrid.

Even after I regained my memories, I held onto the warmth he gave me as hope, I waited for him to tell the truth to me, but he twissted it even further. I continued to call him Vincent not to keep it a secret that I knew him, but to reasure myself that, that... he wasn't lying.

Maybe my memories deceived me, maybe he was Vincent, but no more, not after I know his truth and what he did to me.

CHAPTER ELEVEN

VINCENT.

Astrid sat there, his hands limp, head bowed like some marionette left without purpose. There was blood dried at the base of his nose. His skin was pale, too pale. Not from fear. From what I'd been giving him.

He looked up the moment the lock disengaged.

"So, Astrid," I said, stepping into the room slowly, deliberately. "How's life treating you?"

His lips twitched, a broken attempt at defiance. His jaw clenched, but the tremor in his limbs gave him away.

"Y-yo—u spi-k-ed o-ur..." The words stumbled out, tongue heavy, jaw rebelling. "C-coward... Fl-ower..."

I smiled. "Oh, please. Don't flatter yourself. It's just your method. I learned from the best, didn't I?"

His eyes widened. Whether it was fear or disbelief—I didn't care. He deserved both.

"I asked you something, Astrid." I pulled the chair across from him and sat, folding one leg over the other with quiet grace. "Project Salient. Why?"

He blinked, slowly.

"Don't bother trying to answer," I added casually. "Correction—I won't let you."

I picked up the syringe from the silver tray beside me. He didn't even flinch. Maybe he couldn't anymore.

"This," I said, tapping the glass like it were champagne, "is just mercury. Nothing fancy. But then again, you know how it works, don't you?"

I drove the needle into his arm with elegance. He jerked, ever so slightly. His breath caught.

"This will make sure you feel every second, Astrid. No blacking out. No drifting into unconsciousness. No comfort of a scream. Just you. Just me. Just silence."

I leaned in closer, close enough that my breath ghosted across his cheek.

"Soon, you'll be paralyzed. But not quite yet."

He tried to speak again. I watched, fascinated, as his tongue failed him.

"Oh, don't look so surprised," I whispered. "This isn't the first time. I've been dosing you for the past week. Every little opportunity. A little in your coffee. A little on your skin. I know you don't go to hospitals anymore. You thought that was clever."

I stood again and circled him like a snake warming itself around prey.

"You always hated being touched, didn't you? Hated hospitals. Hated needing help. So easy to slip something in. So easy to make it look like weakness was yours alone."

He blinked. That was all he could do now.

"You were always the strong one, weren't you? The one who told me not to cry. The one who taught me to lie better, to kill cleaner, to vanish faster."

I crouched beside him.

"But you forgot one thing, Astrid. You forgot that pain remembers. And mine? Mine grew teeth."

He tried to move his fingers. Nothing. Only the slow, terrible rise and fall of his breath betrayed his panic.

"I don't need you to talk," I murmured, eyes locked to his. "I just need you to listen."

And in that frozen stillness, I began.

"2005," I said quietly.

He didn't move. Couldn't. But I watched his pupils shift, react. Good.

"The year you rescued me," I mocked. "No—kidnapped me. From my mother. After murdering her."

His eyes didn't blink.

I stood, pacing now, voice building like a storm rolling in. "You always called it a rescue. A blessing. 'You owe me your life, Isa.' You said that. Over and over. As if you were some kind of savior."

I stopped in front of him.

"But I remember now."

His breath stilled. That was enough.

"You weren't saving me from her," I hissed. "You were saving me from the truth."

I knelt beside him again, not with tenderness—but with fury buried in every syllable. My voice cracked, not from weakness, but from rage years in the making.

"I remember the bruises. The belt. The perfume. I used to think it was my mother who hit me. Her voice, the silhouette in the hallway. The humming."

I swallowed, slow and sharp.

"But it wasn't her, was it?"

I waited.

"You made me believe it was," I whispered. "But it was your mother. Your mother. The one who raised us both. The one you called a saint."

His fingers twitched.

"You let me believe my mother beat me. That she was the monster. You told me she was dead because she deserved to be. But she didn't beat me, Astrid. She held me."

I was trembling now, not from fear—but fury.

"You murdered her," I spat. "And then rewrote my grief. You rewired my mind to love your mother—the woman who carved lines into my back like I was furniture."

I stepped back and stared at him.

"She beat me, and you let her. And when you couldn't stand seeing the damage anymore, you killed the woman who was trying to protect me, and called it mercy."

He tried again to move, to speak, to explain. But I didn't let him.

I walked to the tray and picked up the second syringe. It glinted under the low light like a promise.

"You don't get to explain now," I said softly. "You had years."

And then I whispered, so quietly it almost sounded like a prayer:

"You turned me into a ghost of my own childhood."

I turned back to face him.

"And now, I'll return the favor."

"You might think it's funny," I said, voice low, bitter, "how a child who served you for years—worshipped you, feared you, detested her own mother for beating her—suddenly remembered it all."

His head lolled slightly toward me. His lips trembled like he wanted to say something, but the mercury had long stolen his words. Good. He didn't deserve them.

"But you know what, Astrid?" I went on, stepping closer, syringe still glinting in my hand. "I was made to forget it all. *Not by accident. Not by trauma. But by you. By your hate. By her hate. By the cold, calculated evil you called progress.* You stripped me of every memory that didn't serve you."

I knelt again, right by his ear.

"My mother"s love," I hissed. "Her touch. Her voice. Her warnings. Everything before I entered this monstrous world built by you and your father was erased—" I looked at him tilting my head to a side slightly, "- *That was* **Project Salient.**"

His eyes widened, even through the paralysis. The words hit. He knew I knew now.

"That name still burns, doesn't it?" I laughed quietly, almost fondly. "Salient. The great awakening. The experiment. The cleansing. The place where you turned children into weapons, and called it progress."

I leaned in, lips just beside his ear now.

"But here"s the part you didn't calculate, brother—*you forgot what happens when a weapon so strong ...starts to have a mind of its own.*"

I rose, looked at the needle again, then back at him.

"This one's not for you," I said. "This one's for her. My real mother. The one you stole from me, and buried beneath your lies."

I uncapped the syringe and whispered.

"Let's see how much truth your body can hold."

"I thought twins were quite similar," I said, pacing slowly in front of him, the chains around his wrists clinking softly with every breath he took. "But you and Vincent... you were poles apart."

I stopped, turned to face him.

"He cared for me," I said, quieter now. "Adored me. Protected me—even when he shouldn't have. Even when I didn't deserve it."

I crouched in front of him, letting the syringe dangle lazily between my fingers like a pendulum of promise.

"And the sad part?" I tilted my head. "He wasn't as cruel. Or as stone-hearted as you. Was he?"

Astrid didn't move. Couldn't. But his eyes said enough. They always did.

"You... you didn't protect me," I whispered. "You reprogrammed me. Broke me. Built me into something to serve you. And then when that wasn"t enough, when I started asking too many questions, you erased me."

I stood again, slowly.

"And- Leo, you and him were the creators of Project Salient, weren"t you" - "Don"t worry I didn"t forget Eve."

"You and Vincent," I began, circling him like a vulture picking at memory, "were twins. From Father"s second marriage."

I stopped beside him, close enough that he could hear the hatred beneath my breath.

"But then Vincent disappointed you, didn't he? He had a heart. He looked at me like I was human—not some experiment wrapped in skin. He couldn't be your weapon. Or your test object. So you needed me."

I crouched down slowly, leveling my gaze with his, eyes like knives, voice like frost.

"And you chose me the moment you saw what my silence could do. What fear had done to me. I was perfect. Malleable. Yours."

I stood again, pacing toward the steel table, fingers grazing over the stained pliers, the old files, the tray of used syringes.

"And Eve..." I smiled, but there was no joy in it—only revelation. "Eve was my mother's niece. We didn't know back then. But you did, didn't you? You recognized her the moment you saw her."

I turned to him again.

"She was yours before she was ever mine."

My voice dropped to a whisper. "So all that warmth she gave me? All the hugs,the sleepovers, the whispered promises at night—that was all for show. She spiked my coffee, my drinks with Propfol for hallucinations and memory haze, during our time together"

"Sometimes, I feel I should let Aaron survive, he atleast didn't hid the past, and he helped me get rid of Evelyn, even though he considered her a sister, he killed her, for *me*, because she hurt me, then used it against me'-"that was wrong to use it against me but I already knew by then so its fine.'

"I would've let him live but, I can't overlook his sins over his goodwill'

I clenched the edge of the table until my knuckles whitened.

"Evelyn- she wasn't family. She was a plant. A mirror. A knife wrapped in comfort."

I walked back to him, kneeling slowly so he could see the fury in my eyes, sharp and focused, not hysterical. Not anymore.

"You took my mother. You turned her niece against me. You made me believe the wrong people hurt me... while the right ones bled trying to save me."

I leaned in close, my voice now trembling, not from weakness but the sheer weight of what she"d carried for too long.

"Do you understand, Astrid? You didn't just raise a weapon. You created a storm. And now, you don't get to tell the story anymore."

The truth was I lost my memory twice, once after Project Salient and second, by the gunshot.

Christmas Eve. Two Years Ago.

The email came with no sender name. Just an emblem—twisted, thorned, familiar. NSSA.

I hadn't meant to open it. Just like I hadn't meant to remember.

But I did.

Project Salient. Eight of us—once seven—fed drugs that stripped memory like skin, trained like soldiers, engineered like machines. Propofol. Scopolamine. Mercury. Military commands embedded like viruses. No past, no family—just handlers and orders.

And I followed them. For years, I obeyed. I thought I owed my brothers everything. Thought they saved me.

But they built me. Bent me. Broke me.

And tonight, the truth was bleeding under my skin.

But the only thing Aaron delibrately made up was Vincent being involved in this. That's why he had to die.

The basement was colder than usual. The bulb overhead flickered, casting shadows that danced just out of rhythm. Vincent sat on the old iron chair. Astrid stood behind him—arms folded, posture casual, eyes sharp.

Like he was waiting for something.

I stepped in. Quiet. Tense. The door slammed shut behind me, unprompted.

Vincent looked up first.

"Lilith," he said. Voice soft, cautious. Like he knew.

Astrid smiled faintly. "Didn't think you'd show."

"You knew," I whispered. "You both knew what they did to me."

Vincent's brows furrowed. "Lilith, I—"

"I trusted you," I hissed. "You let me live a lie."

Astrid stepped forward slowly, blocking half of Vincent from view. "You're angry. Understandable. The truth is heavy." He tilted his head. "But perhaps it's better you found out this way. Clean."

"Project Salient," I spat. "Your father's masterpiece."

He didn't deny it. "It worked, didn't it?"

My hand trembled near my coat pocket. The weight of the gun felt alive. I hadn't planned to bring it. I just didn't feel safe anymore—not even with them.

Astrid took another step forward, tilting his body—just enough to obstruct Vincent again. Just enough to make me focus only on him.

"I remember now," I said. "You—your mother. Not mine. The woman I thought hurt me—she was yours. You stole me. Made me forget my mother loved me."

Astrid blinked slowly. "Correction," he said, voice calm. "We made you forget."

Vincent tried to speak, but Astrid cut him off with a single look.

That's when I noticed. The faintest motion—Astrid subtly pressing his boot behind Vincent's chair leg. Blocking him from moving. Pinning him in place.

I didn't have time to think.

Because Astrid leaned forward just slightly and whispered—

"She wanted to give you up."

It wasn't true. Not anymore. I remembered now. My mother begged. Screamed. Fought for me. She didn't give me up—he took me.

I snapped.

The gun was in my hand before I even registered it. The rage turned red, blurring the edges of my sight. Astrid's smirk, his control, his lies—they were everything wrong in my life. The barrel rose. My finger tightened.

Astrid shifted again. Slight. Measured.

And Vincent moved—

Right into the path.

The shot rang out.

Time slowed. Then shattered.

Vincent gasped, stumbling backward. His hand flew to his chest, now soaked in red. He fell—hard—his head hitting the edge of the chair before slumping to the floor.

The silence after was deafening.

I blinked. Realized what I'd done. Dropped the gun.

"Vincent?" I crawled to him. "No. No no no—Vincent—"

His eyes fluttered, searching mine. He tried to speak, but blood bubbled at his lips. I cradled him, my hands stained crimson.

"I didn't mean to—" My voice broke. "I thought—Astrid—"

Vincent's fingers weakly gripped my sleeve. He whispered something I'll never forget:

"He...moved me..."

And then his hand fell.

Astrid's voice came from behind, low and smooth.

"Well. That's unfortunate."

I turned, fury rising through my grief, but Astrid only tilted his head, watching me like I was a puzzle he'd just finished solving.

He said nothing more.

Because he didn't need to.

He'd wanted this.

Vincent was in the way. Too soft. Too loyal. Too much like family.

And Astrid knew exactly how to make me pull the trigger.

Then before I could do anything to help Vincent or kill Astrid, he shot me in the head.

I fell to the ground beside Vincent.

And, handed me white chrysanthemums.

Back to the present.

I took Aaron and Astrid and made them sit parallel to each other—two shadows once indistinguishable from the men I called brother, friend, god.

Leo was killedd, what? I have my men.

But not tonight.

Tonight, they were subjects. Witnesses. Graves.

The chair legs screeched as I dragged them into place. The room—windowless, bare, humming with anticipation—felt like a theatre of reckoning. Cold light pooled in circles on the floor like halos over the damned.

Their faces were bruised. Blood still sticky on Aaron's temple. Astrid's lip split open like a red smile. Neither spoke anymore. Not after what I'd done to their hands.

And still... their eyes. One full of rage. One full of regret. Both cowards.

The old grandfather clock in the corner struck midnight.

Twelve, slow, echoing chimes.

I closed my eyes.

And pulled the trigger.

The bullet tore through air and time, a single line connecting the past to the present. It entered through Astrid's head—sharp, clean—and exited into Aaron's skull like a whisper.

Two heads. One bullet. One curse undone.

Their bodies slumped, almost gently. Like they'd simply gone to sleep beside each other.

I opened my eyes.

"Merry Christmas," I said softly, looking at Astrid first, then to Aaron, and then to the shadows behind them. "Vincent. Mom. Sunshine."

My voice didn't tremble.

They had taken her from me—my mother. They'd stolen my brother, sunshine and repainted them into monsters in my memories. They'd taken me, over and over, in ways I was only beginning to understand.

Now, I had taken something back.

From the folds of my coat, I pulled out a rusted pin—A small pin. Polished silver, shaped like a serpent coiled around a dagger. I'd seen it before—once—on the lapel of a man who spoke in riddles and never gave a name.

I turned it over. Engraved on the back was a number.

2410

My birth date.

It was from Sunshine the day he died in my apartment, was the day he came to tell me the truth but he couldn't so he slipped this under the couch. He knew this could've happened. His death was also caused because I was living in Eve's relatives' - Aaron's apartment, to which I was unknown.

And a small paper slip.

The one that little girl from Eloise gave me in the red scarf it said "Serpent and Dagger- Betrayal from loved ones "

I walked over to the cupboard behind them, then I pulled out the White Chrysanthemums Bouquet and took it with me.

I unscrewed the cap from the gasoline can I'd brought earlier—no one had noticed. No one ever noticed anything if you smiled right.

I poured it in wide arcs. Around the boiler. Over the stacks of rotting crates. Across the carpeted steps. The smell was thick, nostalgic in a sick kind of way.

My fingers were steady.

In my other hand, a matchbook.

Eloise's, again. Of course.

"The snake never forgets."

That's what was printed on the front. In gold. Like it mattered.

I struck the match.

It flared, then steadied. A single whisper of orange in a world so full of red.

I crouched low. Touched the flame to the floor.

The fire was almost eager. It leapt like a child finally freed from rules. Crawled up the stairs like vengeance in physical form.

As it spread, I didn't run. I walked.

Room to room. Watching the old place be swallowed whole. The portraits melted into warped caricatures. The wallpaper curled like scorched skin. And above me, I could hear coughing.

Astrid.

Still alive.

But not for long.

I whispered a name. Not his.

Vincent.

Then I whispered another.

"Mom."

And then—
"Merry Christmas."
    Not to them.
To myself.
To the girl I used to be.
To the ghost they created and tried to control.
    The arson wasn't an accident. It wasn't vengeance.
It was liberation.
    I stepped outside just as the house began to howl.Like the walls
were confessing everything I didn't need to hear anymore.
    Snow fell again. Soft, gentle, unforgiving.
    And behind me, the world I once knew turned to ash.
    I took a few White Chrysanthemums out from the bouquet their
at the shutter of the basement, the same place that turned my life
by three- sixty degrees..
    Just like I used to leave it.
    But this time, it wasn't a threat. It was a branding.
    I stood there for a long moment. Then turned away.
    I didn't cry. I didn't look back. I simply walked out of the room,
leaving the ghosts to bleed.
    Christmas, after all, is a time for letting go.
    Interesting isn't it-
    The ones you trust the most,
Could just be as venomous,
Their smiles a mask, their words a boast,
While shadows creep, so treacherous.
    A friend, a brother, all alike,
Their promises like silver blades,
They twist, they strike, when hearts are light,
And leave you lost in silent shades.
    Trust no one, for they wear the guise,
Of love, of care, of friendship's art—
But in their eyes, a cold surprise,
The poison planted in your heart.

I said as I held White Chrysanthemums that were stained by my blood drenched hands.

♫ Playlist ♫

1)-Skyfall – Adele

When alliances crumble and empires fall. Perfect for that moment the betrayal hits and the world shifts.

2)-Renegade – Aaryan Shah

For the loner with blood on their hands and betrayal in their heart.

3)-Breakin' Dishes – Rihanna

Unhinged, raw, and fiery—this one screams "I know you lied to me and now I'm done pretending.

4)-Sweater Weather-The Neighbout

Aaron's betrayal.

www.ingramcontent.com/pod-product-compliance
Lightning Source LLC
Chambersburg PA
CBHW062222150726

47991CB00006B/2398